HUNG LIKE A MURDERER

By that time they had the professor up the thirteen steps. So when the hangman politely waved Longarm ahead of him, Longarm went. When you stepped out on a modest platform one flight up, surrounded by no railings, it sort of puckered your asshole, even if you weren't the one they were fixing to drop. So the effect on Professor Powers was even more dramatic.

He howled, "No! Stop! You can't do this to me! I'm not yet fifty and it seems like yesterday that I was five and nobody had told me I had to die someday!"

The hangman placed the noose over the hood, around the professor's neck, as one of his helpers plucked Longarm's sleeve to move him back a step from the hinge line.

Then nothing happened for a million years as they held the noosed and hooded man steady while he begged, prayed, and bawled like a baby . . .

DON'T MISS THESE
ALL-ACTION WESTERN SERIES
FROM THE BERKLEY PUBLISHING GROUP

THE GUNSMITH by J. R. Roberts
Clint Adams was a legend among lawmen, outlaws, and ladies.
They called him . . . the Gunsmith.

LONGARM by Tabor Evans
The popular long-running series about U.S. Deputy Marshal
Long—his life, his loves, his fight for justice.

SLOCUM by Jake Logan
Today's longest-running action Western. John Slocum rides a
deadly trail of hot blood and cold steel.

BUSHWHACKERS by B. J. Lanagan
An all-new series by the creators of Longarm! The rousing adventures of the most brutal gang of cutthroats ever assembled—Quantrill's Raiders.

TABOR EVANS

LONGARM

AND THE DEAD MAN'S PLAY

JOVE BOOKS, NEW YORK

LONGARM AND THE DEAD MAN'S PLAY

A Jove Book / published by arrangement with
the author

PRINTING HISTORY
Jove edition / September 1997

LONGARM

AND THE
DEAD MAN'S PLAY

Chapter 1

A condemned man wasn't allowed to kill himself. So they'd put a tighter death watch on Professor Powers as soon as they noticed him trying to hang his fool self in his cell. The soon-to-be-late Professor Powers had always been a heap of trouble to the law.

U.S. Deputy Marshal Custis Long of the Denver District Court was reflecting on this as he grumped up the steps of the Federal House of Detention after supper. Pulling death watch could be depressing enough when you hadn't been the arresting officer and a witness for the prosecution. But Longarm, as he was better known to friend and foe alike, had not only tracked the professor down and taken him in alive, if somewhat bruised, but had also gathered the evidence it had taken to nail the slick rascal on a federal murder charge.

None of this weighed on Longarm's mind as he signed in and headed back to the cellblocks to relieve Deputy Smiley. The arrest and the trial that followed had been firm but fair. He just didn't want a man about to die to think he'd come there to gloat.

So as he stepped into the boiler-plate patent cell to find

Deputy Smiley and their prisoner engrossed in a game of chess, Longarm felt obliged to offer them both three-for-a-nickel cheroots and declare in a laconic tone, "You're off duty, Smiley. I hope you understand I tried to get out of this detail, Professor."

The hatchet-faced Deputy Smiley didn't answer. He worked for the same fair but firm boss, Marshal Billy Vail of the stubborn scowl.

As Smiley rose morosely, Professor Powers smiled up at Longarm and said, "I was hoping you might drop by. I've just beat this halfbreed again and you're one of the few chess players I know who can give a man a game."

Longarm smiled thinly down at the somewhat older but still big and husky crook as he replied, "I'd as soon play slapjack and get it over with sooner. I don't reckon I could talk you into sending Smiley here out for a deck of cards?"

Smiley hesitated like a good sport in the open doorway. But their prisoner shook his gray head and insisted, "If I have any choice on my last night with you boys, I mean to pass my remaining time away on a game I'm good at. Do you want to start over, Longarm, or take Smiley's place and superior opening position?"

Longarm didn't answer as he thumbnailed a match head aflame and offered the seated prisoner a light. By the time Longarm had lit the cheroot gripped in his own smile and sat down, Smiley had stepped out into the corridor, the turnkey had slammed the barred door shut on them, and Longarm had sized up the disposition of the chessboard on the top blanket of the fold-down cot he was sharing with the prisoner. So he said he'd as soon save some time by playing out Smiley's game.

Powers said, "In that case it's my move," and moved a black queen to menace one of Smiley's or Longarm's white pawns. Longarm had to take the older man's word on whose turn it was as Smiley's boot heels went off down the corridor towards that waitress gal he'd been sparking of late. Longarm had caught Professor Powers fibbing while

2

they'd played chess in that railroad compartment on the way back from El Paso a few months back. But what the hell, it wasn't as if the one who won this game was going to have his name printed in the *Denver Post*. Reporter Crawford, or the boys from the *Rocky Mountain News,* would doubtless be out back when the time came to write up the big story about a wasted life. But the fact that Professor Powers had been a chess master as well would hardly rate a line.

They didn't call Professor Merlin Powers a professor because he was a master criminal, although he'd been that too in his day. They called him Professor because he'd really been one, teaching business courses at Stanford and dabbling in railroad stocks to prove how smart he was, until the railroading scandals and stock market crash of '74 had wiped out his life savings, inspired his wife to run off with a richer man, and done something mean to his head.

Longarm blew a thoughtful smoke ring as he decided he had no call to waste a move on covering the pawn. Smiley had already moved their white knight to cover more than one pawn, Longarm saw, as the tedious rules of the game came back to him. So he moved his king's bishop one square for no particular reason, seeing he had to move something. He could tell Professor Powers knew he was only making a spit-and-whittle move, because the older man sounded cranky as he snapped, "Pay attention to the game, damn it! It's bad enough to know you're the last son of a bitch I'll ever get to play against. The least you could offer me would be a little concentration!"

Longarm quietly replied, "You leave my maternal ancestry out of this contest or it shall cease forthwith, Professor. I know they're fixing to hang you at midnight, and I don't blame you for feeling a mite upset with me. But my mama had nothing to do with my arresting you, and I'd have never pestered you my ownself if you hadn't shot those federal bank examiners."

Professor Powers sighed and said, "I told you when my

3

bruises healed and I'd had time to think that I understood you were only doing your job, Longarm. As you said at the time, I knew they'd send somebody like you after me as soon as I lost my head like that. Have you any idea why they'll be . . . coming for me around midnight? I always thought we died at dawn. Nobody here has been able to tell me why they've been told to murder me on the stroke of twelve.''

As the doomed felon absentmindedly moved his queen again, Longarm told him not unkindly, ''What *you* did to them two bank examiners could be defined as murder, Professor. You are being *executed* at midnight because that's the way your sentence reads. I didn't write it. Judge Dickerson, down the hall from our office in the Federal Building, has you down for no later than the first of May. Had he written down Mayday morn they'd be coming for you just before dawn, like you'd heard. But Judge Dickerson can be a stickler for detail when he asks whether one of his court orders has been carried out. So we try to carry 'em out to the letter. This being the last night of April, the month of May will commence on the last stroke of midnight. But look on the bright side. You wasn't figuring on getting any sleep tonight, and those wee small hours after midnight can drag like hell. I know this because I have pulled more than one such death watch.''

Professor Powers replied softly, ''Speak for yourself. This is my one and only experience with a death watch, but speaking as the guest of honor, I assure you I'm in no great hurry to get it over with!''

They both heard the cell door opening as Stubby Sheen, the boss turnkey who'd let Longarm in, called out, ''We've been wondering if you changed your mind about that last supper, Professor. It's getting cold out front and it sure smells fine.''

Professor Powers smiled crookedly and replied, ''Why don't *you* eat it then? Anyone can see you're underfed and I've somehow lost my own appetite this evening.''

4

The short aptly named jailor asked if they'd both at least go for some coffee, seeing a whole pot of it had been sent over from Harvey's with all that swell steak, mashed potatoes, and raisin pie with cheese.

The prisoner shook his head. But Longarm allowed he'd go for some coffee, and maybe some of that pie with cheese, if they could spare it. So Stubby said he'd fetch them both some.

As he left, Professor Powers muttered murderously, "Stupid fat slob. Ask him a *real* favor and he refuses with that wet-lipped grin of his! So who asked him to order an expensive last meal for me? Let him choke on it for all I care!"

To which Longarm could only reply, "I admire a man with a taste for subtle revenge. Knowing old Stubby as I do, I'm sure he'll just feel dreadful as he's forced to eat an extra supper for you. You say you asked him some other favor, Professor?"

The condemned man made yet another absentminded move with his queen as he nodded and said, "He said it was too late because Judge Dickerson is out of town. But why couldn't somebody contact somebody like the state governor to ask for a stay of execution, damn it?"

Longarm studied the board as he replied soberly, "Stubby told you true about Judge Dickerson and that big political gathering back in Washington Town. As for any state governor granting you a stay, that only works when his state is fixing to execute you. Nobody but Judge Dickerson, or mayhaps President Hayes himself, can call off a federal hanging set for midnight."

Powers made what seemed like a really stupid move, as if to protect one of his own black knights with his queen, while leaving his much more valuable queen wide open to Longarm's king's bishop.

That was something to study on. So Longarm did as he quietly asked what the condemned chess master had wanted

5

to say to the judge who'd told him to die on the first of May.

Stubby Sheen came back with some coffee mugs and a half a pie with a handsome wedge of cheddar cheese as Powers said, "I've had time to reconsider what both you and the judge said in chambers about some of my, ah . . . business associates."

Longarm thoughtfully placed two fingers on that bishop menacing the older man's queen as he declared, "I'm afraid it's a tad late to make that deal, Professor. Judge Dickerson told you he'd lessen your sentence if you'd care to help us out with some names to go with the master plan I'd already exposed, no offense. But you told him to commit a crime against nature with his ownself, and so here you are with less than six hours to go."

Then Longarm let go of his bishop and moved his knight to take one of the older man's knights, figuring to lose his own in an even swap.

Professor Powers blinked and demanded, "Why did you do that? Didn't you see I hadn't had time to cover my mistake in moving my poor queen?"

Longarm chuckled fondly and replied, "You mean you offered me your queen lest I nip your knight's cross in the bud, don't you?"

Stubby Sheen put the tray on the small end table by Longarm as he asked with a wondering smile what a knight's cross might be.

Longarm said, "We ain't got time to go into all the different moves these glorified checkers are allowed to make. Suffice it to say that queen I just spared is considered most valuable because it can move in more directions than any other piece. I took his knight instead to keep him from moving it to this square right here. Knights are only allowed to move in a tricky L-shaped pattern, which a body can lose track of when he's offered something juicier. But had I gone for his queen instead of his knight, he'd have moved his knight where I couldn't get at it, while it would

6

be menacing both my king and my queen at the same time. That's how come they call it a knight's cross. I can vex hell out of you when you see you have to lose your queen to save your king. You ain't *allowed* to let him have your *king* no matter what. The game is over as soon as you have his king checkmated. They call it checkmated when you run a king up a box canyon with no way out, see?''

Then he tasted some coffee and added, ''This is real Arbuckle Brand, Professor. You sure you won't have some?''

The condemned man dryly observed he was afraid it might keep him awake. Then he moved an innocent-looking pawn and announced, ''Checkmate.''

Longarm blinked down at the board, grinned sheepishly, and admitted, ''I swan, you knew all along I'd go for that knight instead of your queen, didn't you.''

Professor Powers graciously conceded, ''You're a lot better than Smiley. What if you were to wire Judge Dickerson in Washington that I was ready to offer him a list of thirteen names and addresses? I told them I expected them to get me off or bust me out, and so it's not as if I owe anybody anything!''

Longarm suggested, ''Give me the names and I'll run like hell for the Western Union with 'em, Professor.''

''And meanwhile the hangman bides word from the judge?'' insisted the outwardly calm but ashen-faced professor.

Longarm was sorely tempted to give his word and break it. For he didn't really care what a lying crook thought of him in the time a lying crook had left. But Longarm knew *he'd* know, along with Stubby, Marshal Vail, and Judge Dickerson, whether he'd broken his word for a higher cause or not. So he wistfully but firmly told the condemned man, ''The hangman doesn't work for me, Professor. Nobody but Judge Dickerson can call him off, and like I said, I can only try my best.''

He flicked some tobacco ash on the cement floor, sipped

7

some more coffee, and added, "We've got less than six hours to work with now. If you expect me to make a deal by wire for you, I'd best send out for a relief man and haul ass with those thirteen names, Professor."

He set the cup aside and took a notebook from an inside pocket of his tobacco-tweed coat. Then he fished a pencil stub from his matching tweed vest and said he was all set.

Professor Powers shook his gray head and insisted he needed a firm promise before he gave a single other crook to the law. So Longarm put his notebook away, and asked who got the white chess pieces and hence the opening move this time.

The older man licked his lips and told him he could have the whites again. And so it went for what seemed a million years to Longarm, and perhaps five minutes instead of five hours to the man he was holding safe and well for his midnight appointment with Miss Justice and Mr. Death. Longarm finally got the condemned man to sip some coffee. But he had to eat all that pie Stubby had left them by himself. He took his notebook out a few more times, and even won a couple of games after ten or so. But the professor hung tough on the last-minute deal he was willing to make in exchange for his own neck. So when along about eleven-thirty they came for the professor, there was nothing Longarm could do but advise him to stand up and walk to the gallows like a man.

But Professor Powers hadn't taken a lick of advice from Longarm since the day he'd been arrested down El Paso way. So the hangman and his two helpers had to haul him to his feet and half-carry him, kicking and screaming, all the way out back to the gallows set up in the courtyard.

Longarm trailed along behind them all as the chaplain led the way, praying for the soul of a man who kept trying to kick him in the ass as he raged at the laws of man and God. Longarm wasn't anxious to see them hang a man he couldn't seem to beat at chess. Longarm was a good sport, and chess was only a fool game. But he wanted to nail

8

those other crooks Professor Powers had been working with, and men had been known to say the damnedest things as they stood there at the last with that hemp around their necks.

Chapter 2

Federal hangings were more tasteful than some. But by court order they had to be at least semi-public, lest some mythmaker intimate that a condemned man had slipped away to a life of ease in Paris, France.

So despite the hour, the enclosed courtyard was crowded with folks who worked for the government, the newspapers, or the night shift at the nearby rail yards. For even a dignified hanging was more interesting than mayflies around a street lamp at midnight.

Had it been up to Longarm, they'd have brought Professor Powers to the gallows at the last possible moment. He was an admirer of old George Maledon, the top federal hangman, who kept things kinder and more sudden over at Fort Smith. Marching a man slowly to his death, or trying to, made for needless distress all around.

Driven fast or slow, eight out of ten men went quietly in a sort of dreamy daze, likely wondering how come they couldn't quite wake up. A few of them swaggered and tried to pretend they weren't scared. Some of them just didn't want to die, and had to be dragged fussing and cussing all the way, like Professor Powers.

As they got him to the foot of the thirteen steps leading up to the platform, the over-educated but husky crook almost broke loose, and paid no mind even when one of the hanging crew clubbed him in the head. As they commenced to haul him up the steps backwards, Longarm moved over to the hangman and muttered, "Let me see if I can gentle him down some. It's early, and with any luck I might still get a few words of sense out of him."

To which the hangman coldly replied, "I fail to see your name on his death warrant, Deputy Long. Are you saying we don't know how to hang the mulish son of a bitch?"

Longarm said soothingly, "Your boys are doing fine at moving him along. I was only hoping to get a few names out of him. It may not show on his death warrant, but he pleaded not guilty, and there's a heap we just don't know about that mad scheme he had to swindle all those banks in El Paso. He killed the two bank examiners who'd figured out what he might be up to before they ever told the rest of us what it was or who else was in on it."

By that time they had the professor at the top of the thirteen steps. So when the hangman politely waved Longarm up ahead of him, Longarm went. When you stepped out on a modest platform one flight up, surrounded by no railings, it sort of puckered your asshole, even if you weren't the one they were fixing to drop. So the effect on Professor Powers was even more dramatic.

He howled, "No! Stop! You can't do this to me! I'm not yet fifty and it seems like yesterday that I was five and nobody had told me I had to die someday!"

Longarm stepped closer gingerly, since they already had the older man standing on the unfriendly side of the hinges running the length of the plank decking. He said, "One name, Professor. Just give me one name and I'll see what I can do!"

"You promise?" the condemned man pleaded, sounding like a little kid as he added, "Please don't let them hurt me! Give me your word and I'll do anything you say!"

11

Longarm growled, "Hold on, damn it!" as the hang-man's assistants finished binding the professor's arms and legs to the pine plank up his back. But they paid neither Longarm nor their victim any mind as they slipped the black hood over the professor's head and shoulders.

The thin black poplin moved in and out as Powers sobbed, "Oh, God, please don't let them do this to me! Don't let me die just yet and I promise I'll be good from now on!"

The hangman placed the noose over the hood, around the professor's neck, as one of his helpers plucked Longarm's sleeve to move him back a step from the hinge line.

Then nothing happened for a million years as they held the noosed and hooded man steady while he begged, prayed, and bawled like a baby.

Longarm cursed as he stood there helpless, staring off past the hanging party at the upturned faces, shimmering in the guttering torchlight of the courtyard. Then, some-where in the night, a church bell commenced to toll.

Longarm moved over to the hangman, who was standing with one hand on the lever while some idiot in the crowd below began to call out the damned numbers of that damned bell. Longarm could see a puddle spreading from around one of the professor's feet as he whispered to the hangman to just drop the poor cuss and get it over with.

He added, "There's nothing on that death warrant saying you have to stand on church ceremony. They started tolling at midnight. Don't that mean you should have dropped him on the first chime?"

The hangman sniffed and declared in an authoritative tone that this was not the first time he'd ever hung anybody. When Longarm allowed they did it better over at Fort Smith, the hangman suggested Longarm ask for a transfer to that federal district.

So, seeing that the prissy bastard seemed to be enjoying his power of life and death, Longarm turned away to stare down at the crowd some more.

He couldn't make out the idiot who was counting loud and slow, but as the count rose to ten, the professor started to keen as if he was a Navajo way-chanter hoping for a cure. Longarm spied a beefy gent in a checkered suit and derby, standing with a hell of an improvement in blue velvet, her black hair pinned up under a silly but sort of pretty spring bonnet that had a bluebird nesting on it. Longarm knew the checkered suit went with Reporter Crawford of the *Denver Post*. He had no idea who the petite brunette might be. Or what she was doing down below. Longarm was not in the habit of escorting young ladies to public hangings. He suspected that might have something to do with his having more female admirers than some fancier-dressed gents with college degrees.

Then he was glad for the momentary distraction as the platform sort of tingled under his army stovepipe boots and seemed to break in two. He'd been paying less mind to the midnight tolling, and suddenly there was old Professor Powers way down yonder at the end of the rope with his own boots barely clearing the ground as he shit in his pants.

The crowd got a clear view, thanks to the federally specified gallows, with the half that swung down in front like a barn door mounted sideways. As the court-appointed medical team at ground level moved in to make sure the poor rascal was dead after stretching all that rope so taut so far below the cross-beam, Longarm saved himself some waiting at the head of the thirteen steps by just hunkering down at one end of the platform to lower himself over the edge, hang full length with his own boots no more than two feet from ground level, and drop.

As he stood there lighting a cheroot with his back to the dangling cadaver of the late Professor Powers, Reporter Crawford and that nice-looking gal came over. Crawford was already sucking on an expensive cigar, and nice gals never smoked in public, so Longarm didn't figure they wanted to bum tobacco off him.

As he ticked the brim of his dark Stetson to the smiling

brunette, the beefy newspaperman introduced her as Miss Glynnis Mathry out of New York State, and said she was writing a book about Colorado. She didn't deny it, but shyly confessed that this had been her first public hanging. Longarm resisted the temptation to ask how many private hangings she'd been to. There was something about those deep blue eyes to make a man suspect they'd seen plenty, as young as the rest of her looked.

Longarm got his own smoke going as Crawford asked if they could drop him anywhere, seeing they had a driver parked out front with their berlin. Longarm knew they didn't pay Crawford enough for him to keep a carriage, team, and driver. So he figured the *Denver Post* had a reason to show their pretty visitor from out of town a fine time in the Mile High City. But all he said was that he was headed over to the unfashionable side of Cherry Creek, adding that his boss had to give him the next day off after sticking him with a death watch.

The book-writing gal from back East shot a thoughtful look at the still-dangling cadaver a few yards away before she said it would depress her considerably to wait out the final hours with anyone at all. Then she added, ''Merlin Powers would have to be a Welsh name from a good way up The Valley, wouldn't it?''

Longarm shrugged and replied, ''He taught school out California way and talked plain American, with a sort of snooty air to it. Might that name of your own be Welsh, Miss Glynnis?''

She dimpled up at him and confessed, ''Three generations back, but I fear you'd never guess that to hear some of my elders carry on. Why do you ask?''

He said, ''You brought it up, no offense. I ain't sure how Welsh folks are supposed to act—when they ain't pure American, I mean. You don't get as many Welsh saloons as Irish saloons or even Chinese laundries in these parts.''

She sighed and said, ''I know. All the girls at Vassar seemed to know how to act when they didn't have Anglo-

Saxon names. The Scotch girls had family tartans and grudges against one another's clans, while the German girls had all these songs and sausages from home. But it's not as much fun to be Welsh, Swiss, or even Danish because they just don't make up sheet music or comedy routines that might instruct such second-generation Americans in how to behave.''

Longarm said he'd always admired folks who simply acted natural. Reporter Crawford asked him what he'd been fussing about with that hangman earlier. You had to watch Reporter Crawford. He was good at his job.

Longarm shrugged and said, ''You covered the trial. So you know we only had him cold on murdering the bank examiners who might have told us what he'd really been up to. I wanted to talk with him some more before they dropped him. In fairness to the hanging crew just now, the death warrant did specify the first of May, and here we are a tad after midnight. So if it's all the same to you folks, I better move it on down the road.''

They didn't seem anxious to stop him. Then Stubby Sheen, the portly turnkey, joined them, handing Longarm a folded sheaf of papers as he explained, ''I thought you might like to look at this, Deputy Long.''

Longarm unfolded the papers, held them up to the flickering torchlight long enough to whistle softly, and said, ''I've got to show these to my boss at the Federal Building, day off or not! Where did he have all this evidence hid, Stubby?''

The turnkey grinned shyly, aware there was a lady present, as he explained, ''He'd hid them, ah, in the last place you'd expect anyone to look. Anyone but a professional who works that cellblock regular, I mean.''

Longarm nodded, and didn't press Stubby further. He also knew there was a lady present, and any lawman worth his salt knew prisoners seemed to think that hiding stuff under the seat of a latrine was something nobody else had ever thought of.

As Longarm put the papers away under his frock coat, the reporter naturally asked what they were talking about. Longarm would have said they were only some letters. But Stubby had to show off by explaining they seemed to be the names and addresses of the hanged man's associates.

Reporter Crawford whistled and said, "We're talking about a real news scoop here, *pard*!"

Longarm said, "Look, I'll cut you in ahead of the other papers if it pans out. In return, I'd be obliged if you'd sort of sit on it until we have some notion what we're dealing with. The professor was a chess master in more ways than one, and for all we know we were *supposed* to find these names."

Crawford agreed it might not be fair to print a crook's name on the front page before you made sure he was a crook. So he said they had a deal, and they shook on it.

By this time they'd taken Professor Powers off the end of the rope and flung open the side gate of the courtyard so the crowd could move out. As the guards started snuffing torches to speed things, Longarm told Stubby Sheen he aimed to write him up for finding the papers whether they panned out or not.

He lost track of Crawford and the writing gal from back East as the light got less certain. He didn't care. He'd already told Reporter Crawford he didn't need a lift, and climbing into a luxury berlin with a build like that encased in blue velvet could be considered cruel and unusual punishment for a man on his salary.

But as he drifted out the side gate with the crowd, he suddenly saw that she seemed to be drifting beside him, and her French perfume was mighty cruel at close quarters too. Longarm took the cheroot from between his teeth and said, "Howdy, Miss Glynnis. Where might Reporter Crawford be?"

To which she demurely replied, "Let him get his own girl. I'm with you, and now you're going to tell me all about those bank robbers you mean to arrest and hang by the neck until they are dead.''

Longarm laughed uncertainly and told her, ''It's up to Marshal Vail to say whether he wants anybody arrested. Then a judge and jury has to say whether they hang or not. I just work here, for less than they pay top newspaper reporters. That's how come I don't have my own carriage waiting out yonder, ma'am.''

She shrugged her velvet-covered shoulders and pointed out that he'd already said his place wasn't too far to walk.

He got rid of his cheroot to offer an arm he might not need for the .44-40 riding cross-draw under his coat between them, even as he warned her, ''I'd be a liar if I said I didn't enjoy your company, Miss Glynnis. But I just don't have any spare guest quarters at my rooming house, and even if I did, it's after midnight and my landlady can be a fuss about late-night company.''

Glynnis Mathry clung to his arm with both gloved hands while she suggested calmly as anything, ''You'll just have to sneak me up the back stairs then, won't you?''

Chapter 3

The last time things had sounded too good to be true they had been. But this wasn't Nuevo Laredo and she hadn't invited him to *her* place. So what the hell.

His landlady had never really forgiven him for the time he and that other lady had broken through her bedsprings. So it seemed a wise move to suggest a certain hotel near the union depot as both closer and more discreet.

She just clung more cozily to his arm and allowed she'd go along with most anything he said about a town he knew way better. So that was where he took her, feeling good about himself but still puzzled about *her* until she told him, as they strode down a dark deserted street after midnight, how she'd been hearing a lot about such a "famous adventurer" as him since she'd arrived in Colorado. That was what college gals with inviting eyes called a man with a rep with the ladies, a famous adventurer.

He suspected this was not her first adventure in a second-class hotel when she inspected a potted paper palm across the lobby while he registered them both as a couple of other folks. But when he got her up to their hired room and shut the door against the hall light, Glynnis asked if they could have some lamplight of their own.

He lit the bed lamp with an understanding smile, noting that big old mirror facing the bed from a far wall. He admired well-built gals who liked to admire themselves in the act, even if it did make a man a bit jealous of himself as he watched the object of his desire take it with gusto dogstyle.

Looking forward to the looking, Longarm put his Stetson atop the dresser, and hung his gun rig on a bedpost, then noted she hadn't so much as unpinned her hat yet. As he stepped closer, she stepped back, shot him an awkward smile, and said, "I hope you're not one of those men who just leaps at people like an animal, Custis."

To which he could only reply, "Only half of people. I ain't interested in leaping at men. Am I missing something here? I never asked you to go anywhere with me. You volunteered, no offense."

She sighed and said, "I know. I'm trying to respond to you, but you have to give me time. Couldn't we just talk or something as we get to know one another a little better?"

He raised a brow and peeled off his coat to drape it over the foot of the bedstead as he replied, "What would you care to talk about? I don't see no grand piano or tennis court up here."

Ladies were supposed to sit down first. So that left the two of them standing between the bedstead and that mirror, both looking awkward, as she said, "I don't know. Couldn't we talk about those papers the man they just hung seemed to be hiding from you?"

Longarm sighed wistfully, moved around to take the sheaf of papers from his frock coat, and waved her over to the hotel writing table by the window as he said, "Reporter Crawford didn't have to put us all through this bedroom farce, Miss Glynnis. You heard me offer him what I still consider a fair deal. But since the two of you didn't consider that generous enough, read 'em and weep."

She took the papers he offered her with a puzzled smile,

19

asking what Reporter Crawford had to do with what she hoped to keep as their own little secret.

He sat her down at the writing table and moved the lamp over for her to see better as he growled, "I see you're one of those willful gals who just can't take yes for an answer. I'm letting you *look* at those infernal papers. Feel free to copy them down, if you like. After you do, I'll explain the mistake you and Crawford made with this poor country boy."

She repeated her claim that Crawford hadn't sent her after him, and explained, "He told you I was writing my own book. Laugh if you must. But writing is one of the few careers a woman can follow these days and still compete with you men."

He said, "I've read the efforts of the Bronte sisters and our own Miss Virginia Woodhull, ma'am. Might you be out to write about mooning after dead lovers on the Yorkshire moors, or do you figure women ought to have the vote and practice free love, like Miss Woodhull does?"

She smiled up at him sheepishly and confessed, "I'm more interested in this so-called Wild West we read such conflicting stories about back East. To tell the truth, I haven't found things quite as wild as Ned Buntline and Buffalo Bill would have us believe."

He shrugged and said, "You'd have to unpin that fool hat before a West-by-God-Virginia boy I know got really wild with you. Go ahead and read all the Wild West names on those sheets of foolscap, knowing full well that should you print a single one who doesn't pan out as a real outlaw, he, she, or it can sue the liver and lights out of you."

She glanced down uncertainly, brightened, and declared, "Oh, I was right! I have no idea who these gentlemen might be, but they all have names that one might find in The Valley, look you!"

He asked, "Is that a Welsh accent you'd be trying for, and if it is, do you Welsh folks mean Wales when you talk about The Valley?"

She nodded and explained, "According to a great-aunt who still has the Tongue of Arthur, Welsh and Wales are *Saesneg* or English words. *We* call our old country *Cymru* in private, or just The Valley when we don't care to sound outlandish to outsiders, you see."

He said, "Let's get back to those names striking a Welsh lady, no offense, as names from The Valley. Why would the late Professor Powers be so set on recruiting other gents with Welsh names, and since when have Jones and Williams been Welsh names?"

She sighed and said, "You've no doubt heard that the Irish or people of the Hebrew persuasion are inclined to favor their own. My people are more inclined to put on less of a show while never forgetting who and what we are. The fact that most of you don't know Jones or Williams are Welsh names only goes to show how good we are at the game. If you were English, descended from John, your name would be Johnson or Jackson. We prefer Jones or, further up The Valley, Ab Sion. William began as a Norman name, popular for kings and boys. Williamson would be the English way of boasting of some ancestor named William. *We'd* spell it Williams, or perhaps Ab Gwyllum—"

"Further up The Valley," Longarm finished with a weary nod. "I'll take your word on Welsh surnames, and the notion makes sense as soon as you recall that the James and Younger boys are all related by blood or marriage. Don't you aim to write anything down for Crawford, Miss Glynnis?"

She repeated her claim to be working on her own, and sheepishly confessed she hadn't brought along her notebook. He started to offer her a sheet from his own, but the hour was late and he had to get that list over to the office bright and early. So he took the papers back, put his coat back on, and put them away again as he told her, "We'd best see about getting you to your own hotel now, ma'am."

She almost wailed, "I never set out to seduce those

names out of you! I just told you I didn't even have my notebook with me!''

Longarm moved closer to the door, slipping on his gun rig and hat along the way as he declared, ''I'm going downstairs to buy us a fifth of Maryland Rye to go with that free water in yonder ewer, ma'am. If you want to, you can get undressed and into bed in private. If you don't want to, you don't have to. I ought to be back in about fifteen minutes.''

He ducked out into the hall without waiting for her answer. He'd met up with college gals who'd read too much for their own good on other occasions. He suspected that Miss Virginia Woodhull in her own free-loving flesh might be a chore to get started with. For no matter how much anyone fumed and fussed about the equality of the sexes, men and women were *not* the same, and doubtless deserved something more than one another. For there was more to it than just being concave or convex down yonder. Men knew what they wanted, which was anything they could stick their dicks in that didn't hurt. Women wanted more than any man could give them, when they could figure out what in the hell it *was* they wanted. It didn't seem fair, and a man could hardly blame the poor critters for acting so confounded and confounding a lot of the time. But like most men, he failed to see why they thought it was *his* fault.

Down in the lobby he asked the sleepy night clerk where a man might buy liquor around there at that hour. The clerk suggested an all-night bottle shop across from the union depot. Longarm had been afraid he'd say that. But he knew the place and it wasn't too far, so what the hell.

But once he was outside on the dark deserted street, he had an even better notion. He went across the street, lighting a cheroot along the way, to stand in a dark recessed doorway, cupping the smoke in his curled palm so he could just sort of fade in. For he had almost a full fifth of the good stuff waiting in his hired digs across Cherry Creek, if he aimed to drink alone, and Maryland Rye was a luxury on his salary.

22

So he decided to wait a spell and make sure he hadn't set out on a fool's errand. He smoked the cheroot a good ways down, and was almost fixing to scoot over to that bottle shop for that ice-breaking booze when, sure enough, a petite figure in blue appeared in that old hotel doorway, stared up and down the apparently deserted street as if to make certain nobody was watching, and then moved along the walk toward that railroad depot at a pace a legged-up infantryman would have been proud of.

As he watched her trim figure recede through alternate lamplight and darkness, Longarm sighed and said, "Lord have mercy, her legs must be in great shape under that firm rump. But she means to catch herself a hack home at the depot, and wouldn't the two of you have met awkwardly if you'd been coming back from that bottle shop about now?"

He took a deep drag on his cheroot as he morosely weighed the odds on getting at least some of his money back from that room clerk across the way. He grimaced and decided, "It's bad enough he knows by now that neither one of you are up yonder right now. You're only out the money you'd have been out in any case. So why not just get up from the table and leave the game without crying over the way the game panned out?"

He stepped out of the doorway and headed the other way, idly wondering why you often didn't feel like going home once it got this late at night and your boot heels got to echoing back at you from the somehow more interesting darkness all around.

He knew this part of downtown Denver wasn't all that interesting in the daytime. It was only this dark after sundown because the saddle shops, hardware stores, and such you found this close to the rail yards and stockyards were closed for the night. There wasn't a whorehouse or even a saloon this side of Cherry Creek, and he roomed on the far side of the creek because that unfashionable neighborhood was even duller and hence more affordable.

23

There'd be more action up on Larimer Street, and seeing that the Larimer Street Bridge crossed Cherry Creek . . .

"Forget it!" he warned himself sternly out loud. He kept his words inside his skull as he added, "The Blake Street Bridge is two blocks closer, and a man looking for action along Larimer at this hour is a fool with a hard-on who's more likely to wind up with a hangover and less pocket jingle by the time he gets this list of suspects over to the damned office in the morning!"

So he headed on home alone, vowing he'd give the story to those less pesky reporters from the *Rocky Mountain News,* if and when there *was* a story.

U.S. Marshal William or Billy Vail of the Denver District Court raised that point when Longarm joined him unusually early after a restless five hours of sleep, a cold shower, and a change of cotton.

As the two lawmen blew smoke at one another the next morning in Vail's oak-paneled inner office at the Federal Building, the older, dumpier, and balding lawmen read off the thirteen names from the papers spread across his already cluttered desk and declared, "Seven out of a baker's dozen ain't bad. We have a Texas wanted flier on file to go with this Bran Williams from Slagtown, Texas, which is only a short ride out of El Paso, where Professor Powers killed those bank examiners. Jones, Morgan, and Richards are so common they sounded made up when we had them over at the House of Detention a spell back. I'd have never remembered a Jack Jones, but a Gower Jones sort of sticks in one's mind. Rhys Morgan was run in on suspicion of robbing the U.S. mails, as I recall, and I forget what we were holding Taffy Richards on. Ain't Taffy a dumb name for a boy?"

Longarm nodded, but said, "I heard one time that Taffy is Limey slang for a Welshman. That might mean the one called Taffy Richards was born in The Valley, as they call it. What about those other six names the professor wanted

24

to swap us had we been able to swap that late in the game?''

Billy Vail shook his bullet head and said, "Never heard of 'em, and you could be right about it all being a game. Powers was a stuck-up high-strung confidence man. These names I recognize all go with roughnecks. Had he had even this one Texas hardcase at his beck and call down El Paso way, he'd have never had to murder those bank examiners to begin with! So doesn't it seem more likely he'd just memorized some other crooks with Welsh names? My name is Scotch, and so I tend to notice when I meet up with others of the same persuasion. That doesn't mean I plan to rob a bank with the Reverend Campbell or run away with Neighbor Duncan's wife. Professor Powers might have only been funning with these names. When a man's stalling for time, one crook's name is as good as any other. Since it didn't *help* him, who's to say?''

"Bran Williams of Slagtown, Texas." Longarm replied, adding before his boss could object, "It's not too far aboard a D&RG southbound, and like you said, a short ride aboard a federal bronc from the fort. So how's about it? I can get down and back in no time, with or without Williams, depending on whether he's there or not.''

Billy Vail snorted in disgust and snapped, "How often do you find a wanted killer at his last known address, old son?''

Longarm shrugged and replied, "Can't say if nobody ever calls on the son of a bitch. Professor Powers seemed sure he was in Slagtown. Is that where the Texas Rangers have his kith and kin?''

Vail thought, scowled, and said, "No. That flier says he used to live in Amarillo before he started shooting folks for a nominal fee.''

Then Vail decided, "*Bueno*. Have Henry type your travel orders and check the D&RG timetables. But I want you to

25

promise you only mean to check on this first name on the list for now. If you don't strike pay dirt on the first try, you come on home and we write Professor Powers off as a desperate bullshit artist, hear?''

Chapter 4

The southbound express to El Paso left Denver in the afternoon to get you there the next morning, Lord willing and the creeks didn't rise. That gave Longarm time to go back home, change into a more sensible blue-denim field outfit, and gather up his McClellan saddle, Winchester '73, and such.

Riding just one night in a coach car wouldn't kill anybody. But it sure could get tedious, and a man just never knew who he might meet in the club car before bedtime. So Longarm made a deal with an underpaid conductor he'd ridden south with before, and booked a private compartment with its own running water and a flush toilet hidden under one cushioned seat.

This being May, the range cows they kept passing were grazing lavender pasque flowers and white sand-lilies. But the view would have been more interesting if the compartments had faced the nearby Front Range to the west. So Longarm read some magazines he'd picked up back at the union depot. He'd asked if they'd had anything about Wales or the Welsh folk. But they'd just looked at him funny. So what Glynnis Mathry had said about Welsh-

Americans feeling left out was likely true. They'd carried two German-American and four Irish-American newspapers in the depot, along with a couple printed in the Greek and Hebrew alphabets.

Longarm had had to settle for a copy of the *Strand Magazine* from London Town, which seemed to be fairly close to Wales. They didn't have anything about Welsh-Americans in the English publication, but he enjoyed two stories, one about Hindu bandits called Thugs and the other a ghost story set in a creepy old manor house just outside of London.

After that he read through the *Police Gazette,* sternly reminding himself that no real gal was built like that engraving of the circus-performing widow of the late James Butler Hickok, who could hardly be that young-looking these days, and probably wasn't even when they'd first married up, come to study on it. Then his growling stomach and his pocket watch agreed it was about time they opened that damn dining car up forward.

As if to prove the point, someone commenced to bing-bong a set of chimes out in the corridor. Longarm had ridden in compartments before. So he knew that was the first call to supper. He left his Stetson on the door hook inside, but wore his .44-40 as he proceeded up the train. If anyone noticed it under the short denim jacket he had on over his hickory shirt, that was their displeasure and none of his own. Billy Vail had told him to be careful going after a known killer, hadn't he?

He had a good lead on the stampede from the coach cars to start with. So when he saw more than one table vacant up forward in the dining car, he strode the length of it to sit with his back to the far bulkhead, able to see everybody else whether they were coming in or already seated. The colored waiter in starched white linen had just handed him a menu and put some ice water in front of him when Longarm spotted a familiar figure coming for her own supper. Glynnis Mathry had a straw boater, sprouting feathers, pinned to her upswept black hair this evening. You couldn't see the color of the dress she had on under that slate-gray travel duster. She seemed to recognize him despite his own change of duds too. So he had to stand up when she came on over to his table, as if she thought she'd been invited to sup with him.

Holding out a gloved hand, she smiled uncertainly and said, "Why Custis Long, whatever are you doing aboard this train?"

He didn't feel like shaking or even kissing her fool hand. So she sat down uninvited when she saw he had no use for it. As he sat back down himself, he said soberly, "I'd ask you the same thing if I aimed to sound green, ma'am. You never wrote down the names of Bran Williams or Slagtown. So either you have a powerful memory, or you already knew who he was or somebody told you they were sending me to pick him up."

She batted her lashes at him and coyly asked if he'd buy her being on her way to interview a Texas Ranger about that dreadful border-raiding Apache Victorio.

When he intimated she had to do better than that, she sighed and confessed, "All right. That nice young man who works at your office told me you'd be taking this train to El Paso, and I just had to see you again about last night, you see."

Longarm shrugged and replied, "Nope. I don't see, no offense. I told you you were free to light out any time you aimed to, and you lit. So what's the story this time? Did the *Denver Post* say they needed all the names on that list spelled right before they'd pay you the money?"

She insisted, "I'm not stringing for that local paper, look you! I'm not hiding the fact that I mean to get a book out of this tour of the West, and I told you I'd heard you were a man who'd be famous as Buffalo Bill and Wild Bill together if he didn't keep warning Ned Buntline and Frank Leslie he'd sue."

Longarm caught the waiter's eye and pointed down at

his menu. As the waiter was coming over Longarm told her, "You can order anything you like if it's on you. If I'm paying for the both of us, you're fixing to have steak smothered in chili con carne with a side order of fried potatoes. You don't want their cream of spinach. It looks like a well-chawed cow's cud. I don't know anyone who's ever *tasted* it. Are you supping with me or not? I don't want you writing about my wild adventures in any book, hear?"

She said she was game for whatever he was having, and told him they never published anything about real people without getting them to sign a legal form allowing it.

He smiled thinly and replied, "I'd heard that. Bill Cody assured me cold sober he'd never given anyone permission to write that whopper about him and the famous Yellow Hand fighting with knives while all their red and white pals covered the action with their repeating rifles."

He gave the waiter their order, ordered the coffee with their food country-style, and turned back to Glynnis to tell her she could ride with him as far as El Paso, but no further. When she wound up to fuss about that, he cut her off with: "It ain't just the simple fact that my boss frowns on my getting ladies killed. There's some dry, dusty riding involved before I even get out to Slagtown, and Slagtown ain't the sort of place I'd want to escort a lady. They ain't used to any ladies who ain't for sale cheap."

She said she'd always wanted to see a really wild Western town.

He said, "No, you don't. If ladies liked towns that way, Denver would still have plank walks and unpaved streets betwixt the state house and the union depot. Towns out this way spring up crudely, then die or grow more refined, depending on whether folks stay or not. Ned Buntline has the winning of the West all wrong. It ain't striking color, beating back Mister Lo, the poor Indian, or filing the first homestead claims that wins new country. The country is won as soon as they build the first schoolhouse and pass a public ordinance against shooting at crows inside the city limits.

You ladies don't really want things all that wild. So they got most of El Paso street-lit after dark, and you might find all sorts of interesting things about Texas in their public library whilst you wait in town for me. There's a good chance the professor's Welsh pal Bran Williams won't be anywhere near El Paso. So after I check him off the professor's list, we might ride back to Denver together.''

The waiter brought their food. The petite brunette stared down at her heaped plates owl-eyed, and remarked, ''I've never heard of baked beans over a steak before!''

He said, ''They ain't the sort of beans they bake back in Boston. But shove 'em out of the way and just enjoy the way they've spiced up your steak if you don't fancy novelty. You were fixing to explain the new rules of this game to me, weren't you?''

She picked up her fork, murmuring, ''I don't know where to begin. I wasn't playing games last night. I may not be as bold about such affairs as that Woodhull woman you mentioned, but I'm not a blushing schoolgirl either as a rule. So I just don't know what came over me at the last minute, Custis. Maybe if you hadn't left me alone to think in such sordid surroundings . . .''

He smiled thinly and murmured, ''I've lost that way before. That Casanova gent, who wrote about all them gals he'd gotten to act sort of silly, warns on more than one page not to let a gal have the time to think for herself, or a clear run at an unlocked door. But I reckon I was never cut out to be like him.''

She replied soberly, ''I know. You like women too much as human beings.'' Then she tasted her chili con carne, seasoned border-style by a kitchen crew based in El Paso, and gasped, ''*Iesu Gristo! Fy nhafod!* What in the world am I eating?''

He said, ''Chili con carne. I thought you didn't speak Welsh. What else did you just say?''

She washed some steak and chili down with coffee, gasped for breath, and decided, ''I like it. I don't really have the *Cymraeg*. But anyone in my family could manage. Jesus Christ, my tongue! My great-aunt was prone to go on in the language for hours, and some of it rubs off whether you're paying attention or not.''

He washed down some chili and steak as well, making up his own mind about her likely dotty great-aunt. Then he said, ''I doubt I'd ever find as much use for Welsh as, say, Spanish or Lakota, even if I had time to learn enough to matter. But feel free to jaw some at me in Welsh whenever you've a mind to. For to tell the truth, I ain't sure just what more familiar lingo it reminds me of, and it can come in handy to sense the difference betwixt, say, Pueblo and Apache, even when you don't understand a word of either.''

She said in that case she'd thank him to remember it was *Cymru* and *Cymraeg,* not Wales and Welsh. Then she started counting from one to ten as *un, dwu, tair, pedair*— or would have if he hadn't stopped her and suggested they save some for later on before lights-out.

She washed down more supper and confided, ''I've been meaning to ask about that. Is it true we have to sit up all night aboard this train? El Paso didn't look that far away on the map.''

He chuckled fondly as he thought back to other greenhorn gals, and said, ''I don't have to sit up all night. I had the sense to hire me a compartment. Maps can be tricky that way, Miss Glynnis. We've got to get out of Colorado with better than four hundred miles of New Mexico Territory ahead.''

She glanced out at the low afternoon sun and protested, ''That would only take ten or twelve hours on a properly run express train where I come from.''

He shrugged and said, ''We ain't where you come from, no offense. A lot of the tracks ahead wind through rougher country than you seem to be used to. But even if we *could* average thirty or forty miles an hour on this line, would you really want to roll into El Paso at four or five in the

32

morning? We'll get there in time for breakfast at a more reasonable hour, and like I said, I have a compartment and I'm sure we can find room for you."

She hesitated, then quietly asked, "Can I trust you, Custis?"

To which he could only reply, "Trust me to do what? It was your own grand notion to start up with me last night and then chase me aboard this fool train, Miss Glynnis. You'll find me as game as most of my disadvantaged sex. Provided you simply say what you want and stick to it. We both agree you're a woman most men would tend to drool over. But to tell the honest truth, I'm commencing to weary of this kid stuff with a woman grown. Which would you rather have for dessert, apple pie a la mode or cheesecake?"

She laughed weakly, and said the cheesecake sounded faster to put away. She never said whether she was concerned for all the other passengers waiting to eat, or whether she was anxious to be somewhere else.

In any case, they finished supper as the sun was setting over to the west behind the mountains, and he helped her to her feet so he could herd her back along the many cars between the diner and the rear club car. They naturally got to his Pullman car first, and she didn't put up a real fight when he suggested they could watch for the evening star just as well out the east-facing windows of his compartment. He waited until he had her seated inside before he broke out the fifth of Maryland Rye from the saddlebag of his McClellan in a far corner.

Running water and hotel tumblers came with the bedding the thoughtful railroad line provided first-class passengers. So he made them two drinks they could sip as they sat knee-to-knee by the windows on the opposing halves of seats you could slide into a bunk bed whenever you wanted. The blankets, sheets, and pillows rode just above them out of sight. You had to call a porter in for help unless you were an experienced Pullman passenger.

He figured she was when, after they'd jawed less than

an hour in the gathering dust, she shot a shy look at the cushioned seat of the flush toilet and asked if he'd mind stepping out in the corridor a moment while she washed her hands.

He didn't mind at all. He'd been wondering how he was going to excuse himself before all that coffee, rye, and water the two of them had been drinking floated his back teeth away.

He moseyed down to the toilet provided for the second-class Pullman passengers who'd be sleeping more publicly behind canvas drapes in a few hours, and used the pisser to water many a railroad tie at the good time they were making along this stretch.

Then he washed and dried his hands and took his time getting back, knowing gals took far longer to piss, Lord love 'em.

He figured he'd given her a quarter hour when he rapped on the door and heard her shyly inform him it was all right for him to come in now.

So he stepped inside, surprised to see she'd trimmed the one wall lamp. Then, as his eyes adjusted to the tricky light, he saw she'd made up the bunk bed and gotten under the covers, after hanging up her hat, travel duster, and everything she could have been wearing under it. So it seemed safe to say she found a first-class railroad compartment less sordid than a second-class hotel room.

Chapter 5

That same Casanova cuss had put down all sorts of fancy things a man might say at times like these. So Longarm suspected Casanova had made up a lot of his romantic yarns. Longarm had learned from Billy Vail that you could tell how uneasy a suspect might be from the way he babbled, with a cuss who was more sure of himself babbling a bit less. So Longarm resisted the impulse to say she looked lovely in the dark as he hung up his gun and sat down on the cushioned toilet seat to shuck his boots and everything else. Meanwhile she, as if to prove old Billy Vail right, babbled a mile a minute, saying she didn't know what had come over her, asking him what had been in those drinks, and remarking on how pretty the moon was rising over the prairie to the east.

He just got into bed with her naked, and cuddled her some and swapped some spit, until her heaving breasts and darting tongue suggested it was about time to lift the lace hem of her silk chemise out of the way and commence to strum her old banjo. All the while she spread her thighs wider and murmured with her lips against his own that she wasn't the kind of gal who'd let just any man have his wicked way with her.

But once he was in her wickedly, gasping with pleased surprise at how small she felt in every way, the shy little thing was moving her trim hips like an old whore breaking in the nephew of a generous regular customer, as if she meant to have them both come back a lot.

But Glynnis was warmer and wetter inside than any whore could have been. Whores could take up a lot of slack by running a stick of alum in and out down yonder, but it sure left them rough and dry. So he tended to believe Glynnis when she told him he was only the seventh man she'd ever given herself to that way. He was too polite to ask how many men she'd given herself to in other ways when she suggested they try it some more with her on top. Bare tits in the moonlight were an inspiring sight as soon as he got that fool chemise off over her head.

By this time her hair had come unpinned to hang down and brush his bare chest, as she bounced in time with the clickety-clack of the iron wheels under them. He ran a hand down between them to tickle her hot clit lest he come ahead of her again. She moaned in what sounded like Welsh, whether she was fluent in it or not. When he rolled her back over to finish right, with her bare toes running through his hair, she told him he was her *annwyl gariad,* which meant her ''dear lover,'' but he didn't find that out until they'd come some more and lay snuggled tight on the narrow bunk as they shared a cheroot under the covers.

The nights were cold in May at this altitude, and Glynnis said she was glad. She said she hated to get hot and sticky anywhere but between her thighs, and allowed she was still hot and sticky because it made her feel so *uneducated* to just sprawl naked with no blinds down and the moonlight streaming in as if they were shameless members of the working class.

He started to tell her she and Queen Victoria had a lot to learn about ladies they felt too proud to sip tea with. But he'd just told himself some gents talked too much in bed, and he wanted to be fair to Her Majesty. He just didn't know what the Queen of England thought of her working-class women, and it was said she seemed mighty fond of that gruff Highland crofter she'd brought down from Scotland to serve drinks to her in bed. Longarm had noticed, spending plenty of his off-duty time with other folks who worked for a living, that gals seemed more immodest and adventurous at the two opposite ends of Victorian society, with poor gals and rich gals the most willing to get down to good old barnyard slap and tickle. Whores who worked a respectable parlor house and wives married up to bank clerks and such were more inclined to screw with half their charms covered up and call the law on a man who asked them for a French lesson.

Glynnis didn't offer more than some fondling of his limp manhood while he stroked her smooth flank with one free hand and passed the cheroot back and forth with the other. When she started jerking him harder, he pleaded, "Let it set its own pace, pretty lady. I promise it will rise to the occasion on its own just a few more miles along these moonlit rails. Meanwhile, it's still early and we ought to see if we can spread our pleasures to last a spell."

She sighed and said, "I want to come and come and then come some more. I'd forgotten how grand it felt, whether you believe me or not. A published author of my sex has to be very careful of her reputation, lest her male rivals accuse her of screwing the editor."

He chuckled and asked, "Who might a lady author have to screw if it ain't the editor?"

She tweaked his shaft painfully and trilled, "The publisher, of course. He's the one who signs the checks. But I'm not being serious. I really have published more than one travel book without my having to get this familiar with any man I didn't really like."

It would have been juvenile to ask how well she'd liked *him.* So he asked her to talk to him some more in Welsh, repeating what he'd said about wanting to recognize the general sound of the language just in case he heard some-body speaking it.

She insisted she only knew a few words and phrases, the way, say, a second-generation American whose folks spoke French might be able to manage *non, oui,* or *s'il vous plait.* But when she added how most such French speakers usu-ally knew at least a few folk songs they might not really understand, Longarm brightened and asked her if she knew any Welsh folk songs.

She did. She explained he was about to hear a sad song about some Welsh gal who was willing to name the church parish and the old home town she'd be leaving, but wasn't about to name the gentle lover she might never see again.

Glynnis propped herself up on one elbow to stare down wistfully at his moonlit features as she crooned at him through the drifting tobacco smoke.

> *"Ffarwel i blwyf Llangower*
> *A'r Bala dirion deg:*
> *Ffarwel fy annwyl garaid*
> *Nid wyf yn enwi neb."*

The haunting tune was pretty. The words confounded hell out of him. He let her sing on until she'd run down before he told her, "That's a mighty peculiar lingo, no offense. Some of those words sounded High Dutch, others sounded French, and damned if some didn't sound sort of English."

She snuggled down against him again and replied, "Some of the words *do* have the same meaning and sound the same, no matter the spelling. I don't know whether we borrowed some words from our *Saesneg* foemen or it was the other way round, look you. But *ffarwel* does mean fare-well, and a Welshman can drink *coffi,* smoke a *sigaret,* and doff his *het* to a *geneth* before she tells him to jump in the *pwll.*"

He got everything but *geneth,* but correctly guessed that

38

it meant a gal, having been told to go jump in a pool by more than one in his time. But after that it got tougher. Longarm just gave up when she tried to teach him mutated Welsh verbs, or the way Welsh shifted the beginnings instead of the ends of words. He decided the odds on Billy Vail ever sending him to serve a federal warrant in The Valley made it downright unimportant whether Mom and Dad were *Fy mam a'm tad* or *Dy fam a'th dad,* depending on whether you were talking about your own parents or somebody else's. Glynnis said that Welsh grammar seemed a needlessly tedious chore to other Welsh-Americans, and then asked in plain English if he'd ever tried it dog-style.

So he shyly confessed he'd always meant to try that some night with a really romantic partner. And if each knew the other was fibbing, as soon as he got to really humping her with his bare feet on the throbbing deck, they were both too polite, and enjoying it too much, to say so.

So a good time was had by all, and they even caught a few winks in each other's bare arms, narrow as the bunk was, before the train's pause at a way station woke them both to see the day was dawning and a couple of snot-nosed little kids were staring in through the grimy glass at them.

Fortunately, they had the covers up over the brunette's bare tits. But she said she was worried about her baggage now that she'd come enough to consider such mundane matters. So Longarm reached up to haul the blinds down, slip on his boots, jeans, and shirt without the socks or long underwear, and ask her what he was looking for and where.

She said she'd left her overnight bag with the porter of her own car. As he strapped on his gun, she sat up naked and found her own ticket stub in her handbag. The sight inspired him to hurry. For her tits looked even grander in broad daylight, and they could always eat after their fool train rolled into El Paso.

He kissed her, told her not to lose his place, and ducked out into the corridor to go fetch her baggage.

Her coach car was just ahead of the club car, way to the

rear. As he traipsed the whole length of the train, he re-
flected on why a gal might choose to sit so far back on the
train. She'd known, of course, that sooner or later he'd head
for the club car or the diner, bless her sneaky little heart.

Other passengers were getting on and off at the last stop
north of El Paso. So Longarm had to wait until the train
started up again before the porter was free to rustle that
overnight bag out of the pile for him. Seeing he hadn't
given Longarm a hard time about it, he got tipped a whole
quarter. There was something about fetching the underwear
of a frisky gal that made a man feel generous.

He worked his way back to the compartment a bit more
slowly as the train picked up speed and commenced to rattle
and sway some. When he finally made it to his compartment, he rapped to be polite, then naturally went right in,
saying, "I hope you know you ain't about to put anything
on for at least another hour and change, honey."

That was when he noticed Glynnis wasn't there. When
he saw her duster, dress, and all were missing as well, he
tossed her overnight bag on the rumpled bedding and muttered, "All right. She's been carried off by Quill Indians,
or she went somewhere to wash up more thoroughly."

His own saddle, possibles, hat, and denim jacket still
hung just as he'd left them. Indians surely would have
helped themselves to his Winchester saddle gun. So he
wasn't worried as he sat down to light a fresh smoke and
stared at the chaparral-covered hillsides whipping ever faster past the windows. They were making good time by the
time he'd really begun to wonder seriously about old Glynnis. Then he rose with a sigh, cheroot gripped between his
bared teeth, and told himself he was being a suspicious fool
as he searched his denim jacket for evidence. Then a big
gray cat got up to stretch and swish its fuzzy tail in Longarm's innards when he found that list of Welsh-sounding
names missing, along with a Welsh-sounding brunette.

He started to dash out into the corridor. Then he stopped
himself and shut the door some more, muttering, "Don't

run up and down like a poor simp, you poor simp. Let them figure it out. Glynnis already knows what a simp she made of you, getting off back yonder with the damned list you *knew* she was interested in!''

He stripped off the bedding and converted the bunk back to better sitting. It gave him something to do with his hands. Then he got out his toilet kit and spent more time than intended on a whore bath and a clean shave. That still left him plenty of time to sit there, fuming over the perfidity of womankind and the foolish fixes a man could get into by listening to his old organ-grinder. He wasn't hungry. He knew he was never going to want to eat a meal or smile at a woman again.

So once the train rolled into the El Paso yards, Longarm was out of that compartment and standing between cars with his own baggage before they pulled into the station. He'd left the wicked writer's overnight bag to fend for itself, once he'd gone through it to find it only half filled with inexpensive female notions.

He dropped to the platform, with his saddle shouldered, before the train had hissed to a complete stop. Down at the far end, closer to the terminal building, he saw there was some sort of commotion going on. As he strode toward it he reached in his jacket with his free hand to fish out his wallet, unpin his federal badge from the leather with his teeth, and put the wallet away again before he stuck his federal license to tote a gun to his shirtfront. For some of those old boys ahead looked to be Texas Rangers, and he just hated to explain himself while staring into the muzzle of a Walker Colt.

As he moved closer, he saw the object of all the attention seemed to be two spurred boots peeking out from under a canvas tarp. A colored porter was coming towards him with some baggage. So Longarm called out to him, ''I'll bet you a nickel you can't tell me what's been going on down yonder.''

The porter lowered his load to the platform and held out

a palm, replying, "You lose, Captain. Rangers just now had a shootout with two outlaws. One just left for the infirmary in the ambulance wagon. There's a morgue wagon coming for the one you can see from here. Do a Texas Ranger ever tell you to reach for the sky, don't be reaching for your gun!"

As he pocketed the tip, the informative porter added, "Stationmaster say them two seemed to be lurking about since before cock's crow, like they was waiting to meet somebody else. Both of 'em wanted by the law and they hangs around a railroad station in broad daylight, ain't that a bitch?"

Longarm allowed it surely was, and said, "I'll bet you a dime you can't name either one of those poor misguided youths."

The porter said he'd lost again, and told him with a grin, "That dead one you see was named Morgan. The one who ain't expected to live goes by the name of Williams."

Longarm numbly asked, "Bran Williams and Rhys Morgan?"

To which the porter cheerfully replied, "That's them. Rangers say they both papered as hired killers. Rangers say the one they was here to meet might have just got mighty lucky!"

Chapter 6

Longarm was inclined to agree with the porter once he'd joined the crowd around the body, introduced himself, and asked the Ranger in charge for a peek at the body. For he'd never seen the one called Morgan before, and it was only on second glance that he noticed that certain look about the lean and hungry-looking features of what might have otherwise passed for a dead cowhand or stockyard rider.

As he nodded at the Ranger who was holding the blood-stained tarp, Longarm said, "There's this French professor who thinks you can spot a cuss who spends a lot of time in prison because certain faces go with the sort of brains that think more crooked than most. But others opine it's prison life that leaves a man looking so ratty and pinched-looking by the time he's thirty."

The Ranger in charge said he'd noticed the way old cons darted their eyes about and sniffed at the air like rats.

Longarm bent over for the saddle he'd placed on the platform as he declared, "Don't matter whether it's born to them or pounded into them. A lawman just has to sense it when there's a crook in the passing throng. But to tell you the pure truth, I doubt I'd have known this son of a bitch was laying for me before it might have been too late. So remind me to buy that stationmaster a drink before he leaves for the day."

The Ranger in charge nodded at the one holding the tarp as Longarm stood tall with his load. Then he nodded at Longarm and told him, "It's too late. He already left. He dropped by our company on his way home, after pulling the graveyard shift here at this station. He said two suspicious characters had been hanging about the waiting room or out on the platforms as he was waiting to be relieved by the day master. He said when he asked 'em if they wanted tickets or a timetable, they told him to mind his own damn business."

The Ranger who'd dropped the tarp back over the cadaver of Rhys Morgan chimed in. "Since asking folks what they wanted from the D&RG Railroad *was* his business, the stationmaster made it *our* business, and one of the boys recognized Bran Williams at first glance. But it was *this* poor chump who first slapped leather when we told the both of them to freeze. That's how come he wound up with the most lead in him. Williams only took a couple of rounds in the back as he turned to run for it. You say you suspect you were their intended target, pard?"

Longarm shifted the bulky McClellan to a less awkward position and said, "I'd like to see if I can get Bran Williams to confirm it. So I reckon I'd best get on over to that infirmary now."

The boss Ranger, an amiable skinny cuss in a white shirt and high-crowned Stetson, allowed he'd as soon tag along and listen in.

So Longarm toted his saddle inside and left it with their baggage clerk for safekeeping. By the time he had, he'd learned his Ranger pal's handle was Sergeant Brazel, which was neither Welsh nor Brazilian but Irish, with some High Dutch on his mama's side.

Longarm explained his sudden interest in such matters as they walked the short distance to the public infirmary

44

attached to a medical school. The Ranger said he followed Longarm's drift about them finding a list of Welsh names prepared by the Welsh-American Professor Powers. But he just couldn't buy a hanged man ordering a lawman assassinated once they'd hung him.

Striding along the sunbaked streets of El Paso, with the day promising to be a broiler despite the spring date, Longarm explained, "Professor Powers was a chess master who never did anything simple if he could do it too complicated for most of us mere mortals to fathom. He won a chess game off me by convincing me I'd figured he'd made a mistake on purpose. I won't numb your ear about chess playing as long as you'll take my word he was one devious son of a bitch."

Brazel insisted, "Nobody could be tricky enough to order a killing from beyond the grave!"

Longarm nodded, but said, "I can see another way he might have set things up. Let's say he knew there was no way he was going to avoid that rope dance. Let's say it annoyed the hell out of him and he was out to get revenge on me for arresting him down this way to begin with."

Brazel brightened and said, "They told us he'd been arrested by one of you boys for gunning them federal bank examiners. Were you the the one who nabbed the murderous rascal?"

To which Longarm had to modestly reply, "I was, and like I said, he must not have really loved me. So he ranted and raved about that list of names he was willing to swap us for his life. Then he hid it where it was certain to be found, knowing I was the one Marshal Vail was most likely to saddle with the chore."

Brazel insisted, "I can see that far ahead. But how in thunder did he tell his business associates down this way that you would be on your way to arrest 'em if they didn't kill you first?"

Longarm explained, "By thinking ahead. He had plenty of time to wire or, hell, write a letter to those two you

Rangers shot. He knew the date he'd die. He knew we'd find his supposed secret list right after. So he was able to warn his pals, or intended tools, I'd be heading their way by this very morning. Is that the infirmary just ahead, pard?''

Brazel allowed it was. A pretty nursing sister with an ugly frown told them they had to come back during regular visiting hours. Then she saw their badges and said they could go on in, although she went right on frowning.

Bran Williams wasn't in any of the wards. He was still having one last .45 slug dug out of his spine as he lay bare-assed and face-down in the operating theater. A mess of medical students were watching from the seats all around up above. The sunlight through the skylight surely made blood run red. Longarm was no medical student, but he'd been to a war one time. So he knew they were working so hard against hopeless odds to save the cuss only because they hoped the young doctors-to-be might learn something.

The kids all applauded when the head surgeon introduced Brazel as the one who'd provided them such an interesting lesson, and waved the two lawmen closer.

When the Ranger introduced Longarm and asked how the spine-shot cuss was doing, the surgeon murmured, "It's too early to say. Our Mr. Williams is semi-conscious, by the way. You have to keep them on their backs if you want to administer the chloroform steadily."

Longarm asked if he could talk to the obviously dying killer. The surgeon probed the open wound gently, and Bran Williams called him a motherfucker. So the surgeon said, "You can try. I doubt he'll make much sense."

Longarm moved around to hunker some and say, "Howdy, Bran. I hope you understand our mutual pal Professor Powers set us both up dirty."

Bran Williams never opened his eyes as he groaned, "Fuck you. Who in blue blazes might this Powers bastard be?"

Longarm sighed and said, "You got the bastard part

right. He was using you and your pal, Morgan, as his tools to get back at me. He told us your names. He told us you were hiding out down this way. Even if you gents had won over to the station, my own pals and all the lawmen on tap would have known just who to hang for my assassination. Are you really dumb enough to cover up for such a shitheel?''

Bran Williams didn't answer. Longarm understood why when the surgeon fooling around with the man's backbone sighed and said, "Oh, well, you can't win them all. I was afraid that hot lead had cauterized that artery sort of half-ass.''

An assistant trying to stop the bleeding with his finger, as if he thought he was a brave little Dutch boy, asked if there wasn't anything they could do.

The surgeon shrugged and asked, "To what end? Didn't you hear he was going to be hanged for murder from a wheelchair even if we could save him?''

Longarm saw the broken blood vessel had stopped gushing. Williams wasn't breathing either. He shrugged and headed out for some fresh air. He didn't see why Sergeant Brazel wanted to hang around to jaw with that medical team. They didn't know toad squat about any crooked plots. The son of a bitch who could have told them more had died with the exact details close to his vest. Old Glynnis had been right about her own kind hanging tight and sneaky against outsiders.

A sudden sneaky thought hit him, but he walked on along the gray corridor, muttering, "She had a Welsh name too, but she didn't seem upset at the hanging, and even if she had been, how could she have gotten word to Texas outlaws no Eastern gal should have known even if she'd known them?''

He moved on, trying not to think about bare tits in the moonlight as he reluctantly decided, once again, not to wire Denver and have a pretty petty thief picked up when she got off that northbound she was no doubt on in the wee

47

small hours of tomorrow. There was no truthful way to charge her without a mention of bare tits in the moonlight, and it wasn't as if she had the one and only list, thanks to good old Henry and his carbon-paper ways aboard that typewriter.

With any luck the *Denver Post* would run all those names prematurely and without permission. Which would get them in a whole lot of trouble and get that fat bastard Crawford fired.

He wondered idly whether Crawford had been screwing Glynnis while leading her astray in other ways. He decided he didn't want to study on that. A man had no way of knowing what lay ahead, and the here and now passed so suddenly that in the end a life seemed more a parade of memories, good and bad, than anything else. So he liked to keep good memories of pretty gals who said they didn't act like that with just any fat bastard they knew.

He was still thinking about pretty gals when he got out to the drab reception area to catch that frowning nurse with a kerchief to her face and her shoulders shaking as if she was trying not to bawl out loud. When she sensed him there, she turned her back to him and tried like hell to recover.

She might have, if Longarm hadn't moved over to gingerly touch one white sleeve and quietly ask, "Is there anything I can do for you, Sister?"

That busted her wide open, and the next thing he knew she was bawling all over him with her red face buried in his hickory shirt while he admired the way she'd pinned her stiff white cap to her upswept palomino hair. He just held her, as fatherly as anyone could hold a gal with such firm but substantial curves, until she managed to sob, "It's not right! It's inhuman! You can't take dying patients in just to experiment on, as if they were stray dogs!"

He let her fuss some more before he said soothingly, "Dog lovers might dispute you, Sister. Dying folks have to be taken somewhere, and this infirmary does serve a medical school. I follow your drift, and it does seem cold to use old drunks or poverty-struck cancer victims as medical exhibits. But if it's any comfort, that Bran Williams you just admitted was a professional assassin who'd treated other folks a heap worse. They ain't experimenting on him no more, by the way. He just died in the theater. So might I ask you a favor, in the name of the law, Sister . . . ?''

"Armour, Venitia Armour, and my friends call me Vita," she replied. With an uncertain look, she added, "What was that about the name of the law just now?"

He introduced himself and explained, "That spine-shot killer had orders to kill somebody over at the railroad station. So weep no more, my lady, and tell me if he's had any visitors since they brought him over here from yonder."

She wiped her red face dry and protested, "Good heavens. He just got here, and you say he's already dead? Our Dr. Frankenstein can usually keep them alive long enough for more than one pointless but doubtless instructive procedure. Who did you think might have gotten here ahead of you, Deputy Long?"

He said, "*My* friends call me Custis. If I knew who might want to visit a spine-shot killer, I wouldn't have to ask who they might be. What time do you get off here, Miss Vita?"

She brushed a stray strand of hair from her flushed cheek as she replied, "I'm on duty until six, and I already have a late supper engagement, ah, Custis."

He smiled thinly and replied, "My sincere congratulations to your *annwyl gariad,* if I have the grammar right."

She blinked and asked what he meant by any old carriage. So he laughed and said, "I just wanted to make sure Armour wasn't a Welsh name. There seems to a lot of that going around lately. I'd be much obliged if you could manage to take down the given names of any and all who might come sniffing about for news of the late Bran Williams."

She gasped, "Good heavens, are you suggesting some

49

other hired killers might drop by to visit with him?"

"Or claim his remains, mayhaps only ask how he is," Longarm replied with a reassuring nod. "Don't worry. Williams and the sorts he used to ride with were professionals. I doubt they'd even be rude to anyone unless they were paid in advance."

She said he'd still scared her skinny.

So he said he'd ask the Rangers to keep an eye on her while he tended to some other chores. He promised he'd come back well before she got off, to keep her company until her beau showed up.

She fluttered her lashes and protested, "He's hardly what I'd call a beau, and it's only a supper engagement, Custis!"

So he waited until Sergeant Brazel joined them, then explained the situation and left whistling.

As he did so, the Ranger turned to the nurse to remark, "He sure seems cheerful all of a sudden. Was it something I just said?"

To which the statuesque gal with palomino hair replied with a Mona Lisa smile, "I'm not sure. It might have been something *I* said."

Chapter 7

It was going to cost them a nickel a word. But Longarm figured he ought to wire Billy Vail the latest news about Bran Williams and Rhys Morgan.

While he was about it, he asked them to wire him a cheaper night letter listing all those other names and addresses Glynnis Mathry had purloined.

He didn't wire them to pick her up when the train she was still on board rolled into Denver. He aimed to question her about her motives when he caught up with her, since making up with a pretty gal could be so pleasant for all concerned.

Then he went to the nearby Eagle Hotel, where he'd stayed the last time he'd been down this way. Once he'd made sure they had him a cheap but decent corner room with cross-ventilation, he ambled over to one of the El Paso banks Professor Powers had aparrently been out to diddle, and had a talk with the manager.

The boss banker had cross-ventilation and needed it, as the West Texas morning heated up. He seemed a good old boy, for a banker, and offered bourbon and branch water along with a claro cigar so they could converse like civilized gents across his quarter-section of desk. All that green blotting paper made Longarm sort of wish they had some pool cues and a snooker game racked up.

For once they got past the latest dead Welshmen and back to Professor Powers, they commenced to talk in circles, the same as the last time. Professor Powers, pleading innocent to the murders of those federal bank examiners, had naturally declined to say what the dead men might have suspected him of, while they, in turn, had been silenced forever by the slick-talking financial genius.

The banker let fly a blue puff of smoke with the observation that the late Professor Powers had been far better at flimflamming others with financial schemes than shooting them in the back.

Longarm sighed and said, "I couldn't get him to admit it, but I suspect he hadn't had much practice at assassination. When you're out to backshoot gents as they're crossing a hotel lobby, it's a good idea to pick a hotel you've never stayed in before. The poor dumb rascal must have figured that bellboy wouldn't remember him from his earlier time in El Paso. But don't never stiff a bell boy at a high-toned hotel with no tip after he's carried two loads of baggage up to your room."

Longarm enjoyed a sip of his fine drink and added thoughtfully, "One of the upstairs maids was able to pick him out of our lineup as well. He'd forgotten the hard time he'd given her about room service. So he'd never paid attention as she reported in for work while he was seated in that lobby chair with a newspaper spread in front of him and a double-action S&W .32 in his lap. But *she* naturally spotted *him* as she passed by, hoping like hell she wouldn't have to make his bed again."

Longarm puffed on the claro and went on. "When you shoot two men in the back at close range, it's best to use at least a .38 Long. When you whore-pistol men en masse, you're likely to leave at least one of 'em in shape to gasp your name as a likely suspect before he croaks. You'd have

52

thought anyone as slick as the professor thought he was would know bank examiners asking about his accounts would have to be suspecting him a mite. But what the hell, if nobody ever made mistakes, the jails and prisons across our fair land would be empty, and then what would I do for a living."

The banker shrugged and said, "I was up Denver way for the trial and, as you say, the double killing was simple to pin on the man. But as you may recall, his lawyer kept trying to convince the jury he hadn't known either victim and had no motive for killing anybody. I admired the way your Denver prosecutor allowed me to testify I'd personally told the professor, him being a heavy depositer, that his account was being audited by those very bank examiners. But as you surely recall, none of us ever managed to come up with just what they suspected him of. The audit ordered after the killings failed to come up with anything illegal. All anyone could ever prove was that Powers had deposited a good deal of money in two separate banks—the other one across the border in Ciudad Juarez, but a perfectly respectable financial institution just the same. You know as well as we know that Mexico imposes a duty on bullion or negotiable paper leaving the country. But Powers allowed his Mexican bank to *pay* the stiff duty on the few funds he transferred to us here in Texas."

Longarm grimaced and said, "We've been over that range with the U.S. Treasury Department, the Texas Banking Commission, and even the Dictatorship of Mexico. He made a bad job of it, but the professor knew what he was doing when he shut those bank examiners up for good. He paid for those murders the other night. So I ain't as worried about the way he meant to diddle two banks on either side of the border as I am about his reasons for killing two men personally."

The banker blinked and said, "I thought we'd agreed he was out to shut them up before they could report what he was up to."

Longarm nodded, but pointed out, "He just ordered, from beyond the grave, two Texas badmen, to lay for me at the station and gun me front, back, or sideways as I was getting off a train."

The banker said, "That's impossible. How could a dead man order another man killed?"

Longarm had been thinking about that longer. So he sipped more bourbon and branch water, then replied, "That ain't the part that has me stumped. The wiley old chess master had plenty of time to write Bran Williams I was coming, likely aboard the most sensible train, before he tricked me into coming by hiding Bran Williams' name and address where it was sure to be found. Williams and Morgan were dumb in their own right. So they got themselves spotted as suspicious characters by lurking too long and too close, lest I get here earlier or later."

Polishing off the last of his drink, he went on. "The part I'm pure puzzled about is why a confidence man with low-rent guns at his beck and call wanted to risk his own neck by going after those bank examiners personally. Neither Williams nor Morgan dressed fancy enough for a first-class hotel lobby as a rule. But they could have dressed for that one occasion, or just waited along the way between this bank and that hotel. So how do you figure the professor trying to do it himself with a toy pistol? And come to study on it, what else might he have wanted with two dumb but dishonest gun waddies on his payroll?"

The banker poured Longarm another drink and served himself a double as he suggested, "Well, we know he must have been planning *something* dishonest as all get-out, and you do rob a bank faster with guns!"

Longarm shook his head and said, "Cole Younger and Frank and Jesse James never opened accounts in that North-field bank and, say, another one across the state line before they rode in with the Miller boys to rob it. Professor Powers was an economist gone wrong. We know he used a different flimflam every time he settled in somewhere just long enough to flim and flam. Most of his slickery seems to have been new angles on old established confidence games. He'd sell a rich sucker a beef herd that wasn't there instead of a gold brick. Instead of a treasure map he'd produce a geological survey showing where he meant to drill for some of that Pennsylvania rock oil here in *Texas,* for Pete's sake. He could lie like a rug. But before he went loco over that bank audit, he never hurt nobody, nor even offered to. Once he got some rich sucker to put up the money, he just took the money and ran. So how in blue blazes do Williams, Morgan, or eleven other mysterious Welshmen fit in?''

He was sorry he'd asked that as soon as the banker wanted to know what Welshmen had to do with recently hung or shot-up crooks. So Longarm finished his second drink to be polite, and hung on to the cigar as he rose and politely replied, ''It might mean nothing. I ain't got the list with me right now, and like I told you before, I have some old ground to go over here in El Paso.''

So they shook on that and parted friendly. Longarm didn't toss the sissy claro aside and light up a real smoke until he was out of sight of the bank. He knew bankers and politicians handed out claro cigars because they smelled expensive and were mild enough for a schoolmarm to light up, should she aim to be polite in turn.

Enjoying his cheap but honest flue-cured tobacco, Longarm strode over to the railroad station, where things were back to dull, and got his McClellan, with his personal possibles and saddle gun, to tote back to his hotel. With more than one train running up and down the mostly single-track line of the D&RG, you could ride either way day or night, and night riding was better between El Paso and Denver most any time of the year. But he doubted he'd be leaving that evening. So it would be best if he changed his shirt and socks, at least, before he met Nurse Venitia Armour and her infernal supper date when she got off at the infirmary. She might or might not have something to tell him about visitors asking about those shot-up outlaws.

Whether anyone showed up or not, Longarm knew it was likely he'd wind up riding over to Slagtown before he headed back to Denver with or without any answers.

He knew he could borrow a federal remount service pony at the nearby army border post. On the other hand, you could usually hire a livery nag for a dollar and a half a week, or four bits a day with deposit.

Better yet, the Eagle Hotel was tied in with the livery across the back alley, and they might not ask for a deposit from a respectable hotel guest. So Longarm circled wide to approach his hotel from an angle you couldn't cover from those corner windows upstairs.

The friendly old Mexican who ran the livery allowed he'd trust any man packing a badge and registered with baggage. So Longarm offered him a cheroot and said he'd come back when and if he needed a mount.

He naturally went across the alley, through a back entrance, and on up the regular stairs to his hired room. The sunlight streaming through a south window and across the hall runner near his corner room made a tiny white match stem shine like a comet against a threadbare blue background.

The match stem hadn't been there when Longarm had left his hired room. He'd wedged it under the bottom hinge of the door as he'd been closing it. It was an easy way to decide whether anyone else had been opening and shutting your doors when you weren't there to watch.

So Longarm lowered his clumsy load to thigh level, and quietly drew his .44-40 as he eased closer on the balls of his booted feet. Doing what he had to do next was easier said than done. He tucked the barrel of his six-gun under his left arm as he gingerly reached for the door knob. When he was able to turn it, silently and swiftly, he kicked the door open the rest of the way as he grabbed for his gun grips and heaved the saddle at the same time.

As the bulky McClellan flew into the room like a big brown bat with its stirrups flapping, Longarm followed in a low crouch with his gun muzzle up and his hammer back. So the two jaspers blazing away in confusion at the flying saddle saw, just too late, that there was no way in hell they'd ever swing their aims his way in time. But they both tried hard as Longarm opened up with fractions of a second to spare.

He nailed the one farthest from him in the chest to shove him backwards through one window, glass and all. *That* shabby stranger was still falling ass over tea kettle down the front of the hotel as Longarm parted the red mustache and yellow front teeth of the nearer target to pile *him* in the same far corner the McClellan had wound up in.

Longarm didn't want blood and brains all over his saddle. So he whipped around the foot of the bed and hunkered down to roll the son of a bitch over and lay his shattered head on the big straw sombrero he'd been shot out from under. The rascal's chocolate-brown and concho-trimmed pants looked Mexican, and his *buscadero* gun rig was nicely tooled with a sort of spinach-and-roses design Chihuahua-style.

Longarm got back up and went over to the window to see what else he'd just been up to. The one he'd pushed out the window with two hundred grains of spinning lead was dressed more Tex but looked more Mex, as far as Longarm could tell from staring down at the figure sprawled on the wood-block paving and busted glass. Despite all he'd just been through the son of a bitch moved one leg as others gathered over him to ask how he was feeling. So Longarm ducked back from the shattered window to tell the other one, "Don't go 'way. Your sidekick is still breathing, and I'd like to hear what he might have to say about this shit."

He got down to the gathering crowd around the sprawled Mexican just as that same Ranger, Sergeant Brazel, appeared from the other direction. Longarm had reloaded and put his side arm away on the way down, but Brazel still said, "Things was a lot less noisy before *you* showed up, Longarm. Did you do this?"

To which Longarm had to modestly reply, "I got another one more thoroughly in my room upstairs. They were laying for me behind my own door. I was about to ask this one why. I have no notion who he might be. Might you?"

The local lawman elbowed some onlookers back from the considerably fallen rider as he grunted, "Yep. He'd be Jesus Gomez of Ciudad Juarez, and I've *told* him no good would come of his pestering folks up our way."

He nudged the bloody denim shirt of the chest-shot Mexican as he added not unkindly, "Howdy, 'Soos. Are you ready to tell us what on earth got into you just now? I know you've always been one mean hombre, but somebody must have paid you a heap to go up against the one and original Longarm, and now you're paying dearly for your mistake. So who got you into this fix, old son?"

Gomez didn't open his eyes as he replied in a sleepy voice, *"Tu madre, gringo."*

That didn't sound Welsh to Longarm. So he repeated that he had another one upstairs.

By this time other Rangers and an El Paso copper badge had elbowed through the crowd to join them. So Brazel told his boys to get Gomez over to the infirmary fast while he viewed some other remains.

As the two of them went inside and up the stairs, with a hotel clerk fluttering after them to make old-maid noises about the Eagle being a respectable hotel, Longarm filled the Ranger in on his short acquaintance with two total strangers.

As they entered his smoke-filled room, the hotel clerk gleeped like a gal who'd just seen a mouse. Longarm said, "Aw, shove a sock in it. I never invited either one of 'em up here, and the government will pay for a new window, seeing it was me as busted it."

Then he asked the Ranger if there was anything to be said for the one on his side near the foot of the bed.

Brazel said, "Sure. That would be another border *bus-cadero* they called Red Cornell, albeit I seem to recall his real first name was Arthur. Might he have been on your list of that professor's Welsh crooks?"

Longarm stared morosely down at the oozing redhead and replied, "We didn't know he was a crook until just now. But he was on that list and the name was Welsh."

The Ranger asked, "What about Gomez? You ain't saying Gomez is a Welsh name, are you?"

Longarm replied, "Nope. But three out of four so far makes this child suspect that list was fairly accurate. Now all I have to do is figure out how in thunder even a chess master could plan this many moves ahead."

Brazel nodded soberly and said, "He couldn't have planned ahead on us Rangers foiling his first ambush. But even if he could, there was no way he could have known which room you'd check into here at the Eagle, or even which hotel you'd choose to stay in this far after they *hung* the slick sneaky son of a bitch!"

Chapter 8

Longarm and the Ranger knew what Red Cornell looked like, and there was no mystery as to the cause of death. So they had no call to ride over to the morgue with the dead rascal. They headed afoot for the infirmary to see if 'Soos Gomez was likely to live.

Nurse Armour told them he wasn't when they stopped at her desk out front. She said, "Honestly, gentlemen, they're beginning to make jokes in the back about you lawmen getting a special price on bullets. Which one of you shot that poor Mexican through his left lung so close to the heart? They say the bullet fractured two ribs and his shoulder blade and they have an awful mess to clean up!"

She looked away with a sigh and added, "The students ought to find it very interesting before septicemia sets in. I've never seen a patient last more than seventy-two hours with a chest cavity full of bone splinters and exposed to our dusty summer air!"

Longarm and the Ranger agreed they didn't need three days to take down a statement if only they got the son of a bitch to make one. But the sawbones had opened him up under chloroform. So they had to wait around for Gomez to wake up.

While they did so, Longarm asked the nurse whether anyone had been by asking questions about the earlier arrivals, Williams and Morgan.

She nodded and said, "Didn't you know? That Mexican you just shot was here with an Anglo earlier. Not long after you'd left, as a matter of fact. The Anglo did all the talking. He said he'd heard we had a Bran Williams here. When I told them Mr. Williams had just passed away, he asked if he might see the body. He explained he'd ridden in the war with a Bran Williams and meant to claim the body if we had his old army pal in the cellar."

"You didn't let him, of course," said Longarm.

It had been a statement rather than a question, but the palomino-haired gal in white said, "As a matter of fact, I didn't have to. He said—I think his name was Mr. Cornwall—he'd never seen our particular Bran Williams before, and allowed he'd simply been confounded by the name both riders had been known by."

Longarm told her, "Cornell. His name was Welsh, not Cornish. He recognized the body of Bran Williams. But that was all he came by for. He wasn't out to bury him. He wanted to be certain he was dead and couldn't give the game away."

Longarm turned to Brazel and added, "Contingency plan. It ain't all that spooky, once you figure how it might have been thought up by a chess master who liked to think way ahead."

The Ranger must have played some chess in his time. For he nodded thoughtfully and said, "Let's say Powers was afraid you'd be too good for the ambush he set up in advance at the railroad station. So let's say he wrote the late Red Cornell you'd likely be coming after *him* if you got by Williams and Morgan."

The somewhat older Ranger frowned thoughtfully and added, "Hold on. I can see Cornell recruiting his Mex sidekick and coming by this infirmary to scout for your trail. But that's where things get sort of fuzzy to this child."

He turned to the nurse to demand, "Did either of them mysterious visitors ask you who shot them boys they just might have known?"

She nodded soberly and said, "I told them I'd heard they'd shot it out with the Texas Rangers and lost. I said I didn't have the names of any Rangers, though. I suggested they read the newspapers if they wanted to know more about riders they said they didn't really know."

The Ranger nodded approvingly, but told Longarm, "Cornell and old 'Soos Gomez didn't come after of *us*. They went after *you*, over to the Eagle Hotel!"

He turned back to Vita Armour to ask, "Might you have mentioned as much as one word about Deputy Long here being in the Eagle Hotel, ma'am?"

She said nobody had asked her a thing about Longarm, and that she hadn't had any idea which hotel he'd be found in.

Brazel shook his head and said, "I knew both them mutts. If they put their heads together tight, they might manage to win an occasional game of tic-tac with a slow learner. They were mean, dumb border bullies and no more. So who told them you'd evaded that first trap and gone to the Eagle Hotel?"

Longarm smiled thinly and replied, "A chess master who planned more than just one move ahead, I reckon. I've been trying to come up with a more likely suspect ever since I caught those killers laying for me at the Eagle. We call what I've been doing the process of eliminating. My boss, Marshal Billy Vail, taught it to me early on when I gave up on herding cows and signed on with the Justice Department."

Brazel asked, "Is that where you separate the sheep from the goats until you narrow things down considerable?"

Longarm said, "It is. I can eliminate the two of you right off because, like you just said, I hadn't told neither of you where I meant to hire a room."

Vita Armour dimpled up at him and said, "Thanks, I think."

He had no call to mention perky brunettes with swell tits to the blonder and more substantial nurse. But he hadn't said a word to old Glynnis about the Eagle Hotel, and even if he had, she was still on board that northbound train. So that eliminated her, Welsh name and all.

He had no call to suspect old Henry at the home office of pointing him out to Texican killers. But even as he thought about his earlier wire to the home office, it felt good to recall he hadn't told them he'd be at the Eagle.

Then it came to him, and he told them, "I stayed at the Eagle the last time I was in town. Me and the professor talked about hotels a heap as I was carrying him north to stand trial for gunning gents in hotel lobbies. I likely mentioned the Eagle as good value for what I get to charge to my expense account. I'll bet that Mex I shot at my hotel recalls getting word from Professor Powers that I'd likely be there if I wasn't on my way to the morgue from the railroad station."

It was just as well neither of them saw fit to bet him money. For when they finally got to talk to Gomez half an hour later, the shot-up cuss handcuffed to the head rail of his iron bedstead in a private room said he didn't know any Professor Powers and suggested they go home and fuck their sisters if their mothers were too busy.

The younger Ranger who'd tagged along to stand guard over their prisoner started to slap his sassy mouth, but Sergeant Brazel told him not to, and suggested, "You can do better than that, 'Soos. We go back a ways, and you know me to be firm but fair with *la raza,* and a man of my word besides."

To which Gomez replied with a lazy-eyed smile, "*No me frieges.* You got nothing I want. So I got nothing *you* want, eh?"

The Ranger replied, "*Que pendejo eres, hombre.* They tell us you ain't likely to make it. We both know you ain't

63

got no kin up on our side of the Rio Bravo. So that means potter's field for your bones, *muchacho*."

Gomez sighed and said, "I never expected to get out of this world alive, and everybody got to be buried someplace, no?"

"The worms crawl in, the worms crawl out," the Ranger insisted in what struck Longarm as a needlessly gloating tone for a cuss who hadn't shot the bastard. But then Brazel added, "Of course, if you was a pal of mine, I could see you was embalmed and sent back to your Mex kin in a lead-lined coffin free of charge."

Gomez hesitated. Then he said, "*Mierda,* with my luck I might not die."

Longarm tried, "The sly old chess master who sent you after me is already dead, 'Soos. You surely know we hung Professor Powers before I ever got here. So there's no way he can get at you, and I hope you can see there's no way he's ever going to pay you anything he told you he might."

Gomez looked up at Brazel and wistfully asked, "Could I have silver handles on that fancy gringo coffin, *viejo mio*?"

Brazel must have been a man of his word. He grudgingly promised, "German silver leastways. We ain't heard your song yet."

The lung-shot Gomez smiled boyishly up at them and declared, "You two ain't so smart. You got a lot of it wrong. Was Red Cornell who said he got a wire from an old pal in the federal jail in Denver. I never knew the *cabrone.* I never saw the wire. But Red said El Brazo Largo there would be coming down to El Paso for to arrest him on an old federal warrant."

Longarm knew El Brazo Largo meant him. But he said, "I never even heard of Red Cornell until this very day, 'Soos! We had federal paper on Williams, Morgan, Richards, Jenkins, and Jones. But we had no notion why the professor had listed Affon, Cornell, Glass, or I forget who all. So I wasn't headed this way to serve Cornell with any warrant, and it looks as if the professor was playing us all for fools!''

Gomez tried to shrug, coughed instead, and said, ''If I had it all to do over again, I might have lived on to become a dirty old man. I had already heard of you, El Brazo Largo. I warned Red you were supposed to be good, but . . . Hey, how did you get that saddle for to fly around your room like that, El Brazo Largo?''

Longarm said, ''Magic. I used to go broomstick riding with this Welsh witch who liked it dog-style. You were fixing to tell me how your pal Red expected to be paid off—by a dead man, I mean.''

Gomez sighed and said, ''*Quien sabe?* Red said he would get out of my way and let me have a certain *mujer linda* we both admired if I would help him for to kill you.''

He added with a sleepy smile, ''You *cabrones* all think you are so smart. I don't know whether Red knew about the price on the head of El Brazo Largo or not. I saw no reason to tell a *pendejo* who thought I would risk my neck for a piece of ass.''

Brazel looked thoughtfully at Longarm, who said, ''Not up here. Down yonder. Some hard losers down Mexico way posted a bounty on me just for helping some Mex pals wipe out a few government patrols.''

The younger Ranger on the far side of the bed laughed and chimed in. ''They say it was a whole artillery column you wiped out in the Baja a spell back!''

Longarm silenced him with a frown and modestly said, ''I had some help, and we were asking 'Soos here about more recent events.''

Turning back to Gomez, Longarm asked how the late Bran Williams and Rhys Morgan had fit in with his plans to collect that Mexican bounty.

Gomez said, ''I didn't know them. Why would I wish for to share the price on your head with *ladrones* I did not ride with, eh?''

Brazel insisted, ''Aw, come on. You and Red Cornell

65

must have compared notes with them other jaspers, seeing you were set to back their play by taking Longarm out if they messed up.''

Gomez insisted he hadn't known any of the bunch but the late Red Cornell.

Longarm told the Ranger, ''I've been assured by others who'd know that even honest Welshmen play their cards close to their vests and don't tell the children what they're up to when they shut the bedroom door. Looking on the bright side, Red Cornell must have felt they was short-handed down this way if he recruited someone who wasn't a paid-up Welshman. I doubt they'd have told old 'Soos here anything he didn't have to know.''

He smiled thinly but not unkindly down at the man who'd been out to ambush him, and added, ''All he was required to do or say was, 'Bang, bang, you're dead.' He's right about them thinking they were smarter. But Lord have mercy, that old con man really made total saps of the the whole bunch!''

He saw nobody there followed his drift. So he explained. ''You had to have been there, but Professor Powers was a sly old dog. I still can't decide whether he acted scared at the last so we'd buy his secret list as a secret list or not. He suckered me in a death-watch chess game by getting me to see a sneaky trick he had in mind and then pulling another sneaky trick entirely. It's too bad, or mayhaps fortunate, he took up a life of crime instead of politics. For he sure was a wonder at making folks outsmart themselves.''

Pointing with his chin at the Mexican he'd had to shoot, Longarm told them, ''He hired four whole gunslicks by mail, without ever putting up one thin dime. Knowing them as fellow knockabout gents instead of followers, he wired them I'd be coming after them, suggesting when and where they might nail me first. Then he left their names and where they might be found for us to think we hadn't been intended to find 'em, knowing my own boss, Billy Vail, would surely send his senior deputy and the professor's arresting officer to look into the fool list. It's possible the late Red Cornell and 'Soos here weren't in too tight with Bran Williams and Rhys Morgan. The professor may have simply kept a list of crooked Welsh-Americans he'd encountered in his travels.''

Brazel pointed out, "Red and 'Soos were by here earlier to view the remains."

Longarm smiled fondly down at the dying Mex and observed, "That ain't to say they'd been told the whole score. I don't like to brag, but if I was setting me up for an ambush by mail order, I doubt I'd ask anyone to lay for a man who'd just walked into another ambush and survived. I'd be more likely to say the son of a bitch was out to get Williams and Morgan, with poor old lonesome Cornell the next on his list.''

Brazel thought and decided, "So would I. I see what you mean by thinking more than one move ahead, pard. But seeing we saved your bacon at the railroad station and put you on the alert at your hotel, I'd say you won. For you're still alive and there's just no way any dead man could know what you mean to do next!''

Longarm sighed and said, "I hope you're right. Old 'Soos here wasn't on the professor's list. So that means only the professor and three of his fellow Welshmen can be eliminated. I still have another ten Welshmen to track down, and he doubtless warned every one of 'em I might be headed their way."

Chapter 9

Longarm settled up at the Eagle and moved over to the Alamo Hotel, hoping the name might not prove prophetic. He didn't see how in blue blazes even a professor named for a Welsh magician had been able to foresee *that* many moves ahead. Longarm had picked his new hotel at random. It wasn't even at the alphabetical head of El Paso hotels beginning with the letter A.

His new digs cost a lot more, but came with their own mighty up-to-date adjoining bath. So Longarm figured it was worth it. He didn't know how long he'd have to hang around El Paso, seeing the Rangers had accepted his deposition on the shootout at the Eagle but had told him not to leave town lest the county coroner ask for more details.

He enjoyed a late-noon dinner at a nearby *cafetin,* or at least he ate some Tex-Mex chili con carne with tuna pie. Chili got less edible as one approached the border, from the north or south, because both Mexican and Texican cooks seemed to think they were having a contest as to who could use the most pepper without actually killing anybody.

As far south as, say, Monterrey or as far north as Amarillo, they got it about right to Longarm's taste. Just hot enough to make your face sweat without leaving scars on your tongue. But since El Paso sat smack dab on the Rio Grande or Rio Bravo, depending on which bank you were standing on, they served their chili silly and meant what they said when they offered hot tamales. The far more soothing tuna pie was made from cactus fruit the Mexicans called *tunas*. It wasn't made out of fish. The coffee was brewed Mexican-style as well. Texicans sure cottoned to Mexican food and drink, considering some of the names they called Mexicans.

When he ambled on back to the Western Union by the railroad station that afternoon, Longarm found his home office had wired him a copy of Professor Powers's list, along with instructions to wrap things up and get on home.

It was just as well he lit a cheroot and scanned the list before he wired back. It saved him an extra message when he noticed one more local address he hadn't accounted for. He tore off a telegram form from the counter pad and wired old Billy Vail that he had to stick around another day or so. He knew it would only worry his poor old boss if he mentioned a sort of sinister neighborhood in Ciudad Juarez.

But he mentioned it later to Sergeant Brazel when he ran into the Ranger back at the infirmary closer to sundown. The palomino-haired Nurse Armour told them both they couldn't pester Jesus Gomez at the moment because he was asleep at last and really needed it.

She explained, "He'll need all the strength we can pump into him with plenty of sleep and beef broth when the inevitable infection sets in."

Neither experienced lawman argued. They both knew how many gunshot victims, military or civilian, were killed more by pus than lead.

Longarm wasn't sure why the Ranger was still hanging around out front. But as long as he was, Longarm told him, "I just got a more complete list of names from Denver. I'd forgot a cuss called David or Dai Jenkins, said to be living in sin with a sweet señorita near the Plaza del Toros in Juarez. He passed through the Denver District Court one time as he was beating an armed robbery charge. Does that mean anything to Texas?''

Brazel nodded soberly and said, ''That's how come he's living south of the border. He shot a man in Slagtown over another sweet señorita. Or mayhaps we should say señora, since she was married to the man Jenkins shot.''

''Sounds like an *hombre muy malo*,'' Longarm decided. ''How about his *cojones*?''

Vita Armour blushed and said, *''Por favor, caballeros! Hablo español!''*

Longarm smiled sheepishly and pointed out that she was a nurse and, if she really savvied Spanish, she ought to know there were a lot of dirtier ways to ask how manly a man might be.

She laughed despite herself and repeated the question to Brazel, using one of the more graphic terms Longarm had reminded her of.

Brazel blushed and replied, ''Dai Jenkins shot that lady's husband in the back. Then forded the Rio Grande by moonlight. We've heard tell since about him and some *other* wife he stole. We've told *los rurales* we'd sure like him back. But they say he ain't done nothing out on the open range they patrol, the *policia municipal* never go into that neighborhood without an army backup, and the Mexican army is out chasing Apache and Yaqui at the moment. But how come you want the rascal if your own district court found him innocent, old son?''

Longarm replied, ''I never said they found him innocent. I said they couldn't prove he'd robbed that crossroads post office because there were no witnesses left alive. You were the one who got 'Soos Gomez to tell us Red Cornell recruited him at the last moment to come after me. How do you like the original plan calling for Cornell and his fellow Welsh-American Jenkins as my intended executioners?''

Brazel nodded. ''I like it a heap. It explains what a mean

70

Mex was doing mixed up with dead Welshmen. It sounds as if Dai Jenkins showed uncommon sense, for him, and flat out refused to cross back into Texas, where he was wanted, to shoot it out with a lawman of your rep. If he stood trial in a Colorado court, he surely must have known more than 'Soos Gomez did about your ways with a gun.''

The Ranger sighed and added, ''It's too bad Dai Jenkins has gotten so smart without reforming his wicked ways. For had it been Jenkins instead of Gomez earlier today, we'd have been able to tidy up that backshooting over to Slagtown whilst we were at it. But there's no way we can get at him as long as he keeps up his regular payments to a certain *rurale* captain we'd like to catch on our side of the border too.''

Longarm said, ''I can't speak for any government officials down Mexico way, but I might be able to bring Jenkins back to you alive once I get the drop on him.''

Both the Ranger and the much prettier nurse stared owl-eyed at him as Brazel protested, ''He's living in that slum betwixt the bullring and them slaughterhouses near the stockyards!''

Longarm said, ''I know. I told you they just wired me some fresh reminders. If I'm right about the late professor's devious chess game, the sinister old sneak doubtless warned Jenkins I had his name and address, without telling Jenkins who'd offered it to us on a silver platter. But as you just suggested, Jenkins declined the bait and Cornell had to recruit outside help. So wouldn't that make you think Jenkins feels he's safe as long as he stays holed up down yonder where he's surrounded by bought-and-paid-for friends?''

Brazel snorted, ''Hell—sorry, ma'am—Jenkins *is* safe from us as long as he stays put in that rabbit warren of 'dobe walls and dusty alleyways. I told you we know where he run to with a Texas murder warrant out on him. Do I really have to tell you why we can't just go down yonder and git him?''

Longarm sighed and said, ''Not hardly. My boss frowns

71

on what they call international incidents too. That's what they call it when you wind up fighting for your life against them homicidal lunatics El Presidente Diaz recruits to enforce his own peculiar laws. But I've managed more than once to make a quiet arrest down Mexico way without starting an all-out second war with Mexico. I'd like a few words with some Mex bankers down that way too. For to this day we don't know for certain what those bank examiners had uncovered before Professor Powers murdered 'em.''

Brazel protested, ''You can't be serious! It ain't as if *los rurales* won't be expecting you, old son! The afternoon editions have already come out, with headlines anyone might read about you shooting it out with Red Cornell, and let's not forget that Mexican national!''

Longarm nodded soberly and replied, ''Might be a tad risky for me to just board the Oñate ferry. But I *wade* pretty good.''

Brazel insisted, ''Damn it, Longarm, you were the one who said they had a price on your head!'' Then he added, ''Jenkins has likely told his shady Mex pals you might be dumb enough to come after him south of the border. It would be like going into a cave after a bear with all the bats armed and dangerous as they wait for you just inside the entrance!''

Longarm laughed lightly, and allowed the Ranger surely painted a comical picture of Ciudad Juarez. Brazel snorted, ''I wasn't aiming to be funny. Don't tell me when and where you mean to jump the border. I got enough on my plate, and when they ask us whatever happened to a certain U.S. deputy marshal, I want to be able to say I can't say with a clear conscience. I'm headed home for a late supper now. Which way might you be headed? Here in El Paso, I mean.''

Longarm allowed he'd stick around and see if 'Soos Gomez woke up, adding, ''I ain't got nothing better to do, and I noticed during the war how wounded and patched-up troopers seemed to come to or fade out in fitful sleep.''

Brazel told him to suit himself and stay out of Mexico as he left Longarm and Vita Armour alone to sort it all out. She rose from her desk as if to share a secret as she told him, "That Mexican is not going to wake up for hours, assuming he ever wakes up again at all. They must have heard about those war-wounded too. They dosed him with enough opium to put a Chinese railroad gang to sleep for the night."

Then she added in a more concerned tone, "You're not going down into Ciudad Juarez alone, are you?"

To which he could only reply, "Looks like I'll have to. You just heard Sergeant Brazel tell us why the Rangers ain't arrested Jenkins yet."

She looked really worried for some reason. So he assured her he'd been down yonder before, and added, "I know the quarter around the Plaza del Toros, Miss Vita. Got chased through it by the Mexican law one night, and may-haps I have a few Mex friends of my own. El Presidente Diaz ain't as popular with the decent folks of Mexico as he lets on with Americano banking and mining pals. So once I get safely across the Rio Bravo, I just might do wonders and eat cucumbers of my own."

She almost sobbed, "You brutes are all alike when it comes to blood and slaughter! Can't you see there are finer things to strive for than domination over other men?"

He nodded soberly and replied, "Sure, I can. But Mr. Rodin is better than me at carving statues and Mr. Edison is better than me at inventing things. So I stick to what I do best, and that just happens to be catching crooks."

She seemed unconvinced. So he said, "I don't get no thrill out of dominating nobody, ma'am. I learned long ago at a place they called Shiloh that it ain't no thrill to kill another poor cuss."

"Then why do you keep doing it?" she demanded.

He was rapidly losing interest in her palomino hair, and even the way she filled out that wilted white linen outfit, as he grimaced and replied, "I thought I just told you. My aim is no more but no less than enforcing the laws of these United States. I ain't out to harm a hair on anyone's head, unless they refuse to come quietly."

She cocked a brow and delicately declared, "*Estas mucho mierda.* I saw the wolfish glint in your eye when you told that Ranger you were going into Mexico after that outlaw, Custis!"

He resisted the temptation to cuss back at a lady who'd just told him he'd been handing her a heap of shit. He just shrugged and said, "Have it your own way. I tear the wings off flies and dunk the braids of schoolgals in inkwells. I'd best be on my way to see if I can find me a dog to kick. You did say somebody was coming by to take you to supper, didn't you?"

She said, "I did, but it was all a mistake. I thought this evening was tomorrow evening. So I suppose I'll be dining alone when I get off in just a few minutes."

Longarm idly wondered if she'd lied earlier to discourage a poor wayfaring stranger, or if she'd sent a message to the local boy she'd decided to move to the back of the stove for now. Half the art old Casanova had written so much tripe about consisted of not saying or asking anything you didn't have to lest you spring a trap in the tangled underbrush of the female mind. So he never asked how come she was free to have supper with him instead. He just asked her out, and she allowed she'd dine with him if he'd escort her home first so she could change out of that uniform she'd spent a whole hot Texas day in.

Five or six minutes, or what felt like as many years later, the night nurse showed up to relieve old Vita, in a much fresher outfit of white linen, which *she* filled right nicely too.

After Vita had introduced him to the slightly younger nurse and taken hold of his arm possessively to step out into the soft light of a spring gloaming with him, she asked in a desperately casual tone what he'd thought of that other gal.

He said, "She seemed nice, and mighty pretty too." Which was the simple truth as soon as you studied on it. But all the way back to her place, an Anglo cottage surrounded by a picket fence in front and a cactus hedge to the sides and back, he got to hear about all the mean things that other gal had done to other gents. So he had a fair notion how things stood between them by the time she'd let him on in and told him she meant to take a quick tub bath before she got gussied up to go back into town with him for some grub.

As she archly indicated a sofa near the one lamp she'd lit up front, Vita said she'd try to hurry since they'd be eating supper so late. Then, as they were standing there awkwardly, she smiled up at him uncertainly and added, "Of course, I could always whip up a simple supper for us here, if you're really feeling anxious."

So he said, "That sounds swell. I was hoping you'd say that."

Then he took her in his arms and kissed her.

She kissed back, thrusting her hips forward in a way that would have felt downright indecent if her legs had been just a tad longer. It felt inviting enough, and as they came up for air, she smiled up radiantly and declared, "That felt swell. I was hoping you'd do that!"

So he asked her in Spanish whether she wanted to be laid right away or after supper. Such questions always sounded more delicate in a lingo you hadn't been brought up on.

She replied in Spanish that she was *muy culo caliente,* or hot as hell, but added that she was all sweaty and sticky.

He assured her *he* needed a bath too, and suggested they take one together afterwards. So she just reached out to trim the lamp, and asked him if he expected a lady to start ahead of him with her poor trembling hands.

Chapter 10

There was a lot to be said for new-fangled indoor plumbing on a warm West Texas evening. There was also a lot to be said for a bare-ass barnyard frolic on the rug with a juno-esque gal who'd gotten sort of pungent since her last bath. For a good deal of the distaste Victorian society expressed toward human body odors was occasioned by the animal feelings such odors had been designed by old Mother Nature to inspire, and Longarm had noticed right off that Vita seemed an unusually emotional gal.

But once they'd rutted like mighty friendly critters for a spell, it felt swell to get in a nice soapy bathtub with her and scrub her back while she sat facing him across his lap to take it deep and soapy. She allowed it felt much nicer than the way she usually took a bath.

They wound up more romantically in her big brass bed-stead, with two pillows under her rump whether they needed them or not.

He'd already noticed she was built broader across the beam than little Glynnis had been the night before, Lord love the both of them. It was sort of awe-inspiring as well as nice to know that, no matter how many gals you got in bed with, there would always be something a bit different. It never ceased to amaze or amuse Longarm how different what was after all no more than empty space, surrounded by a woman, could feel from woman to woman. He didn't ask her how she liked his cock. Gals always assured a man they'd never been cocked better, and when you studied on it, they likely meant it at the moment the question was asked. For even though, looking back, he could recall some ring-dang-doos that had felt better or worse than most, a gal had to be a really dreadful lay to feel less than marvelous when you first shoved it in. For as some kindly philosopher had once written, doubtless in French, nine out of ten women were worth laying, and that tenth one was worth laying for the novelty!

Looking back on his sex life as he hooked an elbow under her knee to either side to probe her some with his second wind, Longarm thought back fondly to that big blonde in Kansas City who'd chased him high and chased him low until she'd dragged him into bed to just lay there like a side of refrigerated beef while he wondered why in the hell she wanted him doing that to her.

There was no wondering with this somewhat smaller but big enough gal. So it inspired him a lot to think back to that frigid ice queen with the torso of a Greek statue while he thrust in and out of the less perfect but passionate depths of another gal who really seemed to like it.

He knew better than to tell Vita he was doing that, of course. So she took his own passion as a compliment, and moaned and groaned under him while she tried to suck him dry with her internal contractions.

He never asked who she might be pretending *he* was while they both went delightfully insane together for all too short a time.

He'd come again, but kept on posting in the saddle lest she think he didn't like her. Then she sighed and said, "We'd better stop for now, Custis. I'm going to need some rock-oil jelly down there if we mean to fuck all night! I

77

know I started this, darling. But to tell the truth, I'm just not used to climaxing more than eight times in a row.''

He thought she'd been faking some to be polite. He never said how many she might be ahead of him as he politely rolled off and asked if she had any idea where on earth his shirt might have wound up.

She snuggled closer atop the covers and replied, ''I think you left it on the rug out front. You only carried your gun-belt and me back here to the bedroom by way of the bath. Were you planning to just fuck and run, you brute? We haven't even had that supper yet!''

He hauled her closer and kissed her pouty lips, then assured her it was going to take a block and tackle to haul him away from her before he screwed her some more. He explained he kept his smokes in a shirt pocket when he wasn't suited up. So she suggested he go fetch his fool cheroots while she rustled up some cold coffee and sandwich fixings. So they parted friendly, with her shaking his organ-grinder, and by the time she came back in with a tray piled high, he was back in bed with a cheroot going good and his six-gun hanging handy. He'd made sure of the front door lock, and she assured him nobody could get at them through her kitchen without making considerable noise.

As she sat beside him on the bed, making sandwiches of ham and cheese on rye, in the nude, with her unbound palomino hair hanging down to let her perky nipples peek through at him, Vita asked if he was always that worried about other men catching him in bed with a lady.

He chuckled and confessed, ''It's happened, but not often. I try not to get in bed with ladies who've been spoken for. You know why else I'm here in El Paso, and they did try for me at the Eagle Hotel earlier.''

He saw he was unsettling her, and quickly added, ''I'm almost dead certain nobody followed us from your infirmary. I've learned to watch for shadows tagging after my own. But you can never have too many door locks betwixt you and the wicked world outside when you have your own mind on other matters.''

She handed him a sandwich, but then she dabbed a little mustard on one nipple and coyly asked if he wanted to taste it.

He did. Most men would have. But after he'd sucked it clean and lain back again with a sandwich in one hand and his cheroot in the other, he asked if they could just have supper now.

They could. She said all that screwing had given her an appetite as well. So they stuffed their faces and sipped some cold but strong coffee before she demanded to know about those men busting in on him and other women.

He cursed himself inwardly and said, ''It was long ago and far way when I was a simple soldier boy and didn't know some married women just couldn't stand it when their own soldier boys weren't about. I forget her name. I'll never forget *his*. For there he was, standing in the doorway in full uniform with his leave papers, when she gasped like she'd been stung by a bee and said, 'Oh, Steve, this is Custis. Custis, this is Steve, my husband.' ''

Vita laughed wickedly and asked who said what next.

Longarm laughed more sheepishly and replied, ''I wasn't there. It was likely just as well for all concerned that I was the first one to come unstuck and get the hell out of that bedroom, grabbing my own stuff on the way and dressing out back in the cornfield.''

He blew a thoughtful smoke ring and added, ''You know, I've often wondered how the two of them finally sorted things out. To this day I don't know whether he killed her, left her, or whether the two of 'em lived happily ever after. I know it left me sweating cold every time it came back to me, for quite a spell.''

''She could have gotten you killed, poor lamb,'' said Vita as she reached for him instead of more ham.

He sighed and replied, ''I just said that. She'd never warned me and my guard was down entirely. As a lawman

I can tell you all too well how many men, and women, have been killed in crimes of passion. That's what they call it when somebody jealous as all get-out kills a false-hearted lover. Or a true-hearted lover to somebody else, for that matter. A heap of folks go *loco en la cabeza* when they start thinking with their *agentes* instead of their brains. The French lawmen have this saying about searching for the female angel whenever they get a killing to investigate. I've found that a heap of folks act desperate over money, but sex, or the lack of the same, can drive folks crazy. So like I said, I try not to fool with gals other gents have first dibs on.''

She assured him she was all his for as long as he could get Billy Vail to let him stay in El Paso. So they got all the chinaware and such out of the way, brushed all the crumbs off the sheets, and tried it dog-style for a change.

He knew she was more experienced at that than she let on when they wound up having a friendly conversation about his future plans, even as she was arching her back to take it deeper that way. Because one of the reasons old pals wound up screwing dog-style so often was the easygoing but delightful pace a couple could set for themselves with the gal resting relaxed on her hands and knees while the gent just stood there, leaning some of his weight on her spread-open rump while he let her have it at a strolling pace. Once the first excitement wore off, but before they were ready to call it a night, a couple could keep going indefinitely dog-style, and tended to, while they just enjoyed the friendly pace, as if they were strolling hand-in-hand, or key-in-the-hole, along a primrose path through a pleasure garden.

She sounded less frantic now as she warned him some more against trying to arrest Dai Jenkins in his own slum neighborhood down Mexico way. She doubtless felt she had a better hold on him now, and it did feel swell, bless her clinging wet innards.

But he made a tactical error when he failed to answer

one way or another. For she sighed, bit down on his shaft pleadingly, and insisted, "You'll never get as far as that terrible slum behind the Plaza del Toros. Sergeant Brazel was right about the afternoon papers. I saw the headlines of that Mexican paper, *La Prensa,* and El Brazo Largo does translate at The One with the Long Arm, doesn't it?"

He pulled her lush rump back, like he was trying to get his toe into a mighty deep sock, and allowed that some Mexican rebels had hung the name on him a spell back, just because he shared their general distaste for the total bastard who'd stolen their revolution from them.

He said, "I know Wall Street admires El Presidente Diaz because of what they call his stable government. I call a government where the little folks get to shovel heaps of *mierda* a stable government too. But you just mark my words. Someday things are going to bust wide open down Mexico way. I think it was Abe Lincoln, or Caligula, who said you could only abuse most of the people for some of the time before they just went loco and bucked you off."

She said, "I'm not trying to buck you off. I'm starting to get hot again and that feels so nice. Those *pobrecitos* will never rise against Diaz and his supporters down Mexico way. And meanwhile, he has a mighty big and brutal police force riding herd on them. If that crazy chess-playing Professor Powers thought he was going to tempt you into crossing the border, *los rurales* will be expecting you to try it for the same reasons, right?"

He started humping faster and friendlier as he calmly answered, "Wrong. You and Sergeant Brazel left two things out. I only talked to two out-of-state newspaper reporters about that list of names. So no matter what they might have read in the local papers, there's no way *los rurales* could know just where in Mexico I'd be headed, whether they know about that Mexican bank and 'Soos Gomez or not."

He got a firmer grip on her ample hips and continued.

"After that, it's a safe bet Dai Jenkins feels he's safe where he is and won't be expecting me."

She asked how come, breathing sort of fast, and so he explained with the wind he had left. "He turned down an urgent request from a pal to nail me first. That would have been way easier on his nerves than waiting for me to come in after him if he expected me to come in after him and . . . Hold on, there's something here I just don't like at all!"

She moaned, "Speak for yourself! I like it! I *like* it! For God's sake don't stop *now*!"

So he didn't, and they both enjoyed it a lot when she fell forward with him inside her to climax moaning and groaning on her tits and tummy with him thrusting hard to keep it in her hard.

Once he got his breath back, he had to assure her it hadn't been what they'd been doing that he hadn't liked.

As they got comfortable with another cheroot in his teeth and her unbound hair all over his chest, Longarm explained. "The professor had a new Mex address on Dai Jenkins. A *secret* one. I have to check some dates with Sergeant Brazel in the morning, but even if Jenkins killed that cuss in Slagtown before I arrested the professor here in El Paso, I don't see how the professor could have known where his outlaw pal ran off to, unless they'd been keeping in closer touch than anyone suspected all the time the professor was planning to shoot a pair of bank examiners."

She started to say she didn't follow his drift. But working at an infirmary in West Texas, she did, and said, "Maybe that's why your old bank swindler had to try the assassination on his own and made a botch of it. He couldn't get this Jenkins ruffian to do it because the Rangers were after him!"

Longarm took a drag on his smoke and pointed out, "Bran Williams and Rhys Morgan were handy a short ride west of town, and he must have known where *they* were or he couldn't have written that down."

She said, "Then he must have been in close touch with

the whole bunch right up to the day he died. So what did he have in mind for them if it wasn't doing his shooting for him?''

Longarm blew smoke out both nostrils and decided, "I'd better ask Jenkins. 'Soos Gomez doesn't really know too much about what the bunch of 'em might have been up to, and Dai Jenkins is the last one left in these parts. So I'm going to ask you to help me get down the other side of the Plaza del Toros and take the rascal alive!''

She protested, "I'm only a girl!''

So he said, "I noticed. I'm glad. I ain't asking you to ride with me down Mexico way. I said I needed your help. I never said I wanted to expose you to any personal danger.''

So she asked him what a nursing sister working for a medical school could do for him and the law.

When he told her she laughed like hell, and allowed that it just might work, but that she thought it sounded indecent and certainly not legal.

He asked if that meant she wouldn't help him do it.

She said she hadn't said that, and suggested he put out that fool cheroot and let *her* try something that could get a body sent to the county jail if ever anybody else found out about it.

El Paso County had strict views on what they defined as crimes against nature.

Chapter 11

The stable government of El Presidente Diaz prided itself on a show of ruthless efficiency. So the Mexican side of the crossing was guarded by four *soldados federales* even though it was siesta time when the rope-drawn ferry-raft nestled against the south bank of the Rio Bravo.

The border guards, sweating in their gray uniforms under the noonday sun, exchanged thoughtful glances as the horse-drawn glass-walled hearse rolled off the planked log raft, with the two hombres seated up front in black with their stovepipe hats, veiled with black crepe, looking almost as gloomy as the mahogany-stained pine coffin on display behind them.

One of the undertakers was a dumpy Mexican. The other a tall sad-looking gringo with some gray in his mustache and sideburns. The lance corporal in command knew it was a dumb question. He still had to ask what they thought they were bringing into Los Estados Unidos de Mexico.

The Mexican undertaker seated beside his Anglo driver held out a typed sheet of bond paper, saying, "The remains of the late Jesus Gomez. You may have read about *los gringos* killing the *pobrecito* yesterday. He wished for to be buried among his own kind. So we are to deliver what is left of him to the Church of the Fourteen Holy Martyrs near La Plaza del Toros. This is the manifesto signed by the gringo authorities.''

Since the *mestizo* lance corporal had been unable to read the newspaper they were talking about either, he waved the typed-up paper aside and declared with the low cunning of the illiterate, ''I spit on your gringo papers. Anyone can put down anything on paper. So let us see what you have in the back, eh?''

The Mexican seated above him protested, ''The casket is sealed. For good reason. You do not wish for to look inside it, El Capitan.''

The flattery didn't work. As his followers drifted closer with more interested expressions and Spencer repeaters, the officious one-striper insisted, ''I have seen dead bodies before. I once saw my own mother lying in her coffin and I did not faint. You think you might frighten me with talk of death, hombre? You think maybe you might be able to smuggle Yanqui rifles to your rebel customers by producing fake papers and telling us you are only delivering dead meat? I am not *asking* you for to show us. I am *telling* you for to show us, and I am telling you this right now, *comprende*?''

So the dumpy Mexican got down from his seat—cursing about the heat, he assured them—while the laconic Anglo on the driver's side steadied the team.

The Mexican undertaker opened the back door of the hearse and rolled the coffin partway out as he protested, ''*Que penejada,* the lid has been screwed down with a dozen *maldito* screws and we are in a hurry. The day grows warm and the body has been hastily embalmed.''

The lance corporal snorted, ''*Sin falta*. Open the *chingado* box!''

So the sweaty-browed undertaker unscrewed the lid and lifted it partway off, allowing the lance corporal and his nearest followers a good look at the mess inside.

85

"*Madre de Dios!* I thought you said they *shot* him!" gasped the lance corporal as the full horror of the naked, pickled, dissected, and partly reassembled cadaver sunk in.

The man squatting on the wagon bed with the coffin lid explained, "He died with no money in the infirmary of a medical school. They told him they would pay his funeral expenses in exchange for *permisso* for to dissect him for their anatomy class. Have you seen enough?"

The lance corporal tried not to gag as he turned away, nodding his head as he managed, "El Gringo has no soul. Get that *cuerpo chingado* out of here, and make sure you do not open that lid for any of his family, no matter how they plead!"

So a few minutes later Longarm and his pal from an El Paso undertaker who catered to *La Raza* were on their way into Ciudad Juarez at a trot lest small boys get too easy a crack at all that plate glass in the back.

As Longarm drove, the Mexican undertaker mopped his brow and marveled, "I never knew I was so brave. But I have to say things went just as you said they might, El Brazo Largo."

Longarm flipped the reins to tell the team which way to turn at a corner and replied, "They call what we just done *misdirection* on the wicked stage where magicians slicker folks. I was told all about it by this magical gal I used to know. Like I told you and your boss back in El Paso, I figured them crossing guards might have been told to expect this child, and I could only change my appearance so much without the stage makeup looking obvious to anybody looking as tight as them boys are trained to look. But as you just saw, they were on the alert for an Anglo lawman, not this hearse and that cadaver we borrowed from that medical school with the help of another magical gal."

The undertaker laughed softly and said, "I would have waited for the real Jesus Gomez to die had I been in your shoes. Did you not tell us his temperature is already rising?"

Longarm shrugged and said, "My pal on the nursing staff says he could last as long as next week, and I'm in a hurry. After that, we need the body to get *back* with."

The Mexican asked, "For why? They will not be expecting El Brazo Largo to be sneaking *out* of Mexico, and what could they suspect us of smuggling across the border in an empty coffin?"

Longarm said, "I ain't sure yet. Meanwhile, that cadaver in the back is so pickled it will keep indefinitely, and I promised a pal I was only borrowing it."

"But what are we to tell them when they ask for why we brought a mangled corpse into their country if we did not mean for to *leave* it there?"

Longarm said, "Let me do the talking if there's any fuss. As you just said, they won't be as suspicious of an Anglo *leaving* Mexico whether he fits my description or not. In the meanwhile, like I said, you and that body will keep safe with Mexican pals of mine down by the Plaza del Toros."

The Mexican living and working in Texas started to ask if they were talking about people mixed up in *La Revolucion*. But on second thought, he didn't really want to know. So less than half an hour later they wound down a narrow alley between high 'dobe walls, and suddenly stopped near a nondescript but substantial oaken gate, where Longarm softly whistled a few bars of "Let My People Go."

He didn't have to whistle loud. Such spirituals were a tad unusual in that particular *barrio,* and someone was always listening tight on the other side of that gate. So the gate suddenly swung open and eager hands reached out to help him steer the team inside, while other hands trained thoughtful gun muzzles their way.

The undertaker from Texas gasped, "*Dios mio,* it's like a military fortress!"

Longarm murmured, "Don't say that too often. This is supposed to be the *pateo* of a house of ill repute. Regular customers ain't allowed back here, even when they're civilians. The madam is an old pal of mine and if you play your cards right, you may spend a pleasant evening here while I attend to other business.''

As they got down from the hearse, a fine figure of a no-longer-young dusky beauty appeared on a balcony above, dressed in red satin and black lace, to call down, ''Ay, Custis, can that really be you? For why are you dressed like a grave digger and for why do you look so *old*? Have you been sick?''

Longarm allowed he'd explain inside. No woman as devoted to the cause of *La Revolucion* as La Conductora, as she was known to everyone but her paying customers, needed more than a hint. So she invited him inside where they could talk more privately.

Longarm left his pal from El Paso in charge of the hearse and its grim cargo and headed upstairs. He knew the way because he'd been this way before. The good old gal's real name was Consuela, but they called her La Conductora in rebel circles because she ran a sort of underground railroad, moving funds, firearms, and friends of her cause this way and that. Longarm wasn't exactly a Mexican rebel, but some of his best friends were down this way. He had a tougher time getting along with the pissants who were running the country officially.

He knocked on the door he'd entered of old, and heard a throaty contralto voice trill, *''Entrade.''* So he did.

La Conductora welcomed him from a horizontal position atop the red satin coverlet of her red-curtained four-poster bed. She'd sure gotten out of her *own* red satin pretty quickly.

But as he approached the sultry temptation, who reminded him a lot of that painting of another naked Spanish lady by Mr. Goya, Longarm felt obliged to warn, ''I'm down here on my own business entirely, Miss Consuela. Nothing I'm asking this time will be of any help in getting rid of your disgusting government.''

She patted the red satin before her tawny torso and purred, ''First *chingamos* and then we talk, eh? For why do you hesitate, *querido mio*? You know I have clean habits and only fuck my friends. Have I gotten that old and ugly since last you visited us with that other *sinverguenza* with the very strange eyes, El Gato?''

Longarm smiled down at her and replied, ''You look just swell to me, Miss Consuela.''

That was true when you studied on it. For while she was a few years older than he was and had a mustache of her own, she wasn't much older than forty, her mustache was only the fuzz you got with a gal that naturally hairy-crotched, and all those curves were as solid as if she lifted weights. Which, for all he knew, she might.

He took off the hat, set it on a bed table, and sat down beside her, wearing his gun under the undertaking suit he'd borrowed. She reached up as if to haul him down to her, laughed, and said, ''*Dios mio*, you have white paint in your hair and mustache.''

He started to explain. But the next thing he knew, she'd rolled him across her as if they'd agreed to wrestle, and had him on his back as she straddled him with her bare things and reached down between them as if to unbuckle his gun rig. But she went for his fly buttons instead, as if she too sensed he was rising to the occasion.

A man could get the feeling he might not be the very first who'd ever passed this way as the beautiful middle-aged brunette shut the curtains for some private screwing at the same time she was impaling her aristocratic torso on his raging erection.

He knew from his last visit that she hailed from an aristocratic pure Castilian clan. She'd bragged about how blue-blooded she was, although if the truth was to be told, those veins you could see through the ivory skin of her Spanish type looked more teal-green than blue. There was another bunch of white Spanish gals whose skin looked more peachy, fuzz and all. The gals like Consuela, who called themselves *sangres azul,* meaning blue bloods, seemed to think that *that* bunch were less high-toned. So he knew he was supposed to feel honored as La Condutora undressed him while she sort of milked his old organ-grinder with her well-broken-in but well-functioning love maw.

He groaned, "Let me get undressed and get on top to finish right!"

But she purred, "Who said anyone here was about for to *finish*? I am almost there myself, *sonrisa de mi corazon*! I wish for to calm us both down to where we can enjoy *el rapto supremo* like adults who are paying attention. I confess that right now I feel too passionate for to more than . . . *Ay, Dios mio, tienes mi corazon en tus manos! Te adoro y chinge me mucho!*"

He knew he didn't have her heart in his hands. She had his cock in her old ring-dang-doo. But since she said she adored him and wanted him to screw her good, Longarm rolled her over and proceeded to do just that while she laughed like hell and said his gun grips felt like they were anxious to screw too as his .44-40 slid up and down the inside of her thigh.

Then they'd both come, and she was right about it being less wild but far nicer once he took time out to strip entirely and start over, slow but deep, with a pillow under her fine old Castilian background.

He tried to converse with her about his other reasons for being down Mexico way, the way he'd been able to screw and talk at the same time with Vita the night before. But a gal who had to concentrate some to speak English had trouble speaking English and screwing as expertly as she wanted to. So when she asked him, moaning, whether he aimed to spend the siesta making love to her or bending her ear, Longarm said they could talk later. For he had no complaints about the way old Consuela made love back to a man.

Likely *any* man, when you let yourself study on it. He

doubted the middle-aged beauty had wound up owning a whorehouse through inheritance from some Spanish grandee.

Not one she'd been directly descended from, leastways. But there was a lot to be said for a retired whore who was doing it with you just for the hell of it. She'd been so right about the delightful ways experienced fornicators could move when they were simply anxious to entertain a guest they admired.

The first time he'd passed through this underground railroad station, he'd wondered whether the madam had taken him under her wing and into this same bed because he was as handsome as she said, or because she'd heard about him shooting those mean *rurales*. Women tended to mix what a man looked like with what a man did for a living, finding both as tempting. It was hard for a man to imagine himself getting a hard-on over a gal because she looked tolerable and sewed buttons back on good as new. But that was the way gals were, Lord love 'em. So he just enjoyed what Consuela had to offer, for whatever reason she was offering, until they were both out of breath and she allowed they could stop and chat a spell if that was his pleasure.

So they did, and finally, he got to tell the queen bee of the local revolution what he had in mind for later that evening.

La Conductora sighed and said, "I won't let you. You are too young and pretty to die and I know that part of town. It would be most dangerous for a gringo after dark if you were only looking for to get laid. If this *malo* you are after knows you might be coming after him, and has his own friends in the *barrio,* you would have less chance than your *pendejo* General Custer had that summer in 1876."

He rolled one nipple between thumb and finger as he thoughtfully said, "I'm in the same spot Custer was. I got to try."

La Conductora quietly replied, ''You are wrong. You are not in the same spot. You are in my arms and I am going for to help you get that *hijo de puta* for Tio Sam and Texas.''

Chapter 12

Mexicans kept odder hours than folks who weren't used to such a hot, dry climate. Settling down for a three- or four-hour siesta in the heat of day, they stayed up later, and got up earlier, to put in about the same twelve hours of work as the rest of their world. So four A.M. was about the best time to creep in on folks in the unlit parts of Ciudad Juarez.

But wanted men sleep lightly, and so David or Dai Jenkins heard the footsteps on the stairs and rolled his bare feet to the floor as he nudged the Indian lady beside him and whispered terse instructions.

Ladies sleeping with outlaws learn to think fast too. So the *mujer* called out in a sleepy voice, *"Quien es? No tengo mi chingado ropa."*

Jenkins was hauling his pants on as a childishly innocent voice called back, *"Telegrafo por Señor Jenkins, señora."*

Jenkins rose to strap on his gun as he whispered, "Play it for time! Nobody I know would be wiring me in these parts!"

So the gal kept her voice sleepy as she called out, *"Sí, sí, un momento, muchacho,"* while Jenkins snatched up his boots, hat, and shirt to roll out over a far window sill half dressed.

He dashed barefoot across the flat roof next door, and tossed his load into the darkness below before he followed a knotted rope down into the same narrow space.

At the bottom he hastily finished dressing, made sure there was nobody staked out in the alley beyond, and broke cover to stroll off at a desperately casual pace. Meanwhile, back upstairs, his *mujer* really had a crumpled yellow telegram from Denver handed to her by the shy-looking street urchin she'd opened up to at last.

She couldn't read Spanish or English, so she failed to see just then that the wire was really addressed to Longarm, care of El Paso Western Union.

Jenkins had planned ahead against a cold gray dawn such as this. So he was headed for his back-up hidey-hole behind the slaughterhouse with increasing confidence as he passed another early riser, looking more like an old Mexican drunk, pissing on the wall just inside the alley entrance.

Jenkins muttered, *"Biendias, viejo,"* and strode on past. But he hadn't strode far before something hard and cold as gunmetal poked him firmly between the shoulder blades and a cold-sober voice warned him to grow roots and grab for some sky if he ever wanted to see the sun come up again.

So just as the sun was coming up, Longarm and his Mexican pal from El Paso were driving that same hearse through that same border crossing, and as luck would have it, that same lance corporal was on duty.

"So what have you for to show me now?" the Mexican trooper demanded in a cynical tone.

Longarm had said he'd do the talking this time. They both knew nobody would be expecting El Brazo Largo to be leaving Mexico, and the impending conversation promised to get tricky.

It did when Longarm said, "The same load as before, only now he's really overdue for his funeral. Seems we delivered the wrong *cuerpo*. Or at least we couldn't get

94

anyone to take it off our hands. You saw before how tough it might be to recognize the poor cuss.''

The lance corporal nodded, but said, ''A most logical story, gringo. But now I wish for to see into that coffin some more, eh?''

Longarm sighed and said, ''Come on, we're in a hurry to unload all that stale meat. We already showed him to you yesterday.''

The officious Mexican insisted, *''Es verdad,* and now you are going to show him to me again. You think I am *estupido*? You think I do not know about the export tariff on silver, or how much silver Mexico exports? Open up, *viejo*! I shall not ask so politely a second time!''

So they unscrewed the lid and let the crossing guard have another look at the same mangled cadaver from the medical school.

The lance corporal gagged. ''Get him out of here! He is starting to bloat!''

So they shut the lid on the horror pressed almost against it now, but didn't screw it down as tightly this time. For they still had to go through U.S. Customs on the other side of the river.

Longarm naturally had less trouble with fellow federal employees he'd let in on the plan. They just went through the motions for the Mexicans watching from the far side. Then they drove the hearse back to where Nurse Armour, Sergeant Brazel, and a couple of more Rangers were anxiously waiting behind the medical school in the early morning light.

Vita ran over to gasp, ''Thank God you made it back! We have to get that cadaver back in its locker so they can give it a proper funeral this Saturday!''

Longarm got down to walk around to the back with her as he said he was glad they treated poor dead folks to a good send-off once they couldn't find anything on or in them worth slicing.

With the Rangers' help they got the cadaver out of the

coffin and wrapped in a tarp to be carried inside like some new carpeting. As Vita supervised that, Sergeant Brazel glanced into the open coffin and asked, "What about Jenkins?"

Longarm reached in to lift the padded false bottom off the less grisly but just as dead-looking Dai Jenkins, saying, "Had some help from Mex friends. I promised 'em I wouldn't go into all the details with anybody they don't know as well as me."

Brazel whistled softly and said, "You're a hard man, Longarm. But mayhaps it's just as well you couldn't bring him back alive."

Longarm shrugged and said, "We got to get that box and this hearse back to its proper owner. Some other Mex pals have promised to wire me a Mex bank statement. I'll be proud to buy you a drink and bring you up to date as soon as I get the time, pard."

So they shook on that and parted friendly. Longarm had never said for *certain* he'd be leaving on the night train to Denver, and he'd never refused to allow the Ranger to feel for any damn pulse. So his conscience was clear when they drove the hearse over to a shack near the railroad yards first.

The Mexican folk she knew there carried the unconscious outlaw inside and stretched him out comfortably on a floor mattress while Longarm handcuffed him to a corner post. Then the *mamacita* served some tortillas and coffee while the *papacito* asked why the other Anglo lay so still if there was nothing really wrong with him.

Hunkered nearby with his mug and snack, Longarm explained he'd had to use some chloroform a pal at the infirmary had given him, lest the man make a fuss about coming back to the U.S. without an extradition hearing.

They thought it was pretty funny too. But when Dai Jenkins came to about an hour later, he called Longarm a son of a bitch and asked him who he was.

Longarm asked the *mamacita* to serve the poor cuss

some coffee for his headache. Chloroform hit you in the head instead of in the guts, like sulphuric ether.

As she did so, Longarm said, "I'm the one the professor warned you against, U.S. Deputy Marshal Custis Long. Before you hand me any bull, I want you to listen tight. Are you listening tight, you poor sucker?"

Jenkins muttered something in Welsh. Longarm didn't ask for any translation. Cussing had a certain ring to it in any lingo, and he didn't want to pistol-whip the owlhoot rider any more than really called for.

Longarm said, "Your mastermind set all you boys up. Knowing full well he was fixing to hang no matter what he offered us, he offered us a list of outlaw names so we'd know it existed. Then he hid it where he knew we'd find it. He was sore at me for arresting him on a hanging charge, and knew I was the senior deputy my boss would send after the rest of you."

"Who's this professor?" the handcuffed outlaw asked.

Longarm snorted in disgust and said, "I told you not to hand me no bull before you'd heard me out. We know that even as he was offering you gunslicks to us, he was smuggling warnings to the bunch of you. He wasn't out to save you from me. He wanted you to kill me."

Jenkins started to protest.

Longarm said, "I ain't done yet. If you try to tell me you never heard of Red Cornell, I'll whup you alongside the head. 'Soos Gomez was taken alive. He told us how Red Cornell had to recruit him when you refused to come after me at the Eagle Hotel the other day."

Jenkins sipped some coffee, shrugged, and said, "What's the charge? I was down in Juarez, minding my own business, when this other lad I barely knew asked if I'd like to help him shoot somebody I had nothing against. I refused. I wasn't there when he talked some greaser into going after his own personal enemy. I told a Mex lawman I know that some other gringo might be planning a crime north of the border. But he didn't seem interested. If you think you can convict me of attempted murder in Texas while I was in Mexico, feel free to try.''

Longarm got out three cheroots, handed one each to his prisoner and the man of the house, and lit his own before he said, ''When you're right you're right. As you likely know, we ain't got any federal paper posted on you right this minute. If I was to take you back up to the Denver District Court with me, they'd likely throw the case out of court and you'd be free to take in a show on Larimer Street in no time.''

Jenkins took a drag on his own smoke and demanded, ''Why don't you cut me loose then?''

Longarm said, ''I'm considering. Got to make up my mind before a slow but sure combination pulls out of the yards for the north this coming noon. Mighty slow train. We'd have plenty of time to chat as we whiled away the time. But seeing you say you don't have much to talk about, I reckon I'd do as well leaving you here in El Paso.''

Jenkins grinned and said, ''I was hoping you'd see things my way. How come you ain't unlocking these fool handcuffs?''

Longarm said, ''Ain't ready to yet. I offered to leave you behind as I headed on back to my home office, outsmarted by you and the late Professor Powers. I never said beans about turning you *loose*!''

He let that sink in before he went on, friendly but firm. ''They tell me you gunned a man in Slagtown, Texas, in the back. That makes it first degree murder in *this* state, old son. It's tough to evoke the *code duelo* when you fail to declare your intentions to a man and give him an even chance. It's even tougher to evoke the unwritten law when it's the honor of *his* wife you're defending at gunpoint. So finish your coffee and I'll be proud to take those cuffs off and march you over to the Ranger post.''

Jenkins paled and protested, ''You can't! You ain't a Texas lawman!''

Longarm smiled thinly and replied, ''Don't have to be.

I don't know how they did it in your old country. But in this country *papacito* here has the right to arrest any known felon, provided he feels up to it.''

Longarm smiled wolfishly and asked, ''Are you trying to say that I ain't up to it, little darling?''

Jenkins whined, ''I don't want to hang for that cold-hearted bitch. She was playing the both of us for hair ribbons and play-pretties. I only found out after I killed her man that she'd been telling him he had a bigger dick than the man *he* took her away from!''

Longarm sighed and said, ''I know the feeling. It's so much easier for them to pretend. But don't talk so dirty in front of *mamacita* here. Save some for me aboard that train, assuming you really want to ride back to Denver with me, I mean.''

Dai Jenkins allowed he was really looking forward to seeing the Mile High City and Larimer Street again. So Longarm left him cuffed, with *papacita* casually holding a ten-gauge Greener on him, for the time it took a man to stroll over to the freight dispatcher's shack across the yards and make a deal to board that freight-passenger combination slated to pull out of the yards around noon, Lord willing and nothing with highball priority needing the tracks to the north.

By working things out that way, Longarm hoped to avoid having to explain his early exit to any Rangers loitering around the regular waiting room and ticket window. Longarm knew there might be a fuss if they saw he was leaving town without clearing it with the El Paso County Coroner. But he'd shot outlaws before, and knew they could get on as well at the hearing without him.

He had no call to go back to the Alamo Hotel. So he never noticed that one Ranger who'd been posted to read papers in the lobby. Old Sergeant Brazel wasn't half the chess master the late Professor Powers, who'd started all this, had been. So Brazel had never guessed Longarm might shift his baggage over by the yards and leave his hotel key on the bed before leaving for Mexico the day before.

It seemed a shame Longarm couldn't say *adios* in a more friendly way to good old Vita. But parting could be a pain in the ass as well as sweet sorrow, and he'd said *adios* tender as hell to old Consuela earlier that morning. He doubted he'd be up to old Vita, or up *for* old Vita, in the near future. So he left town aboard that pokey combination with his prisoner and baggage without saying *adios* to anyone in El Paso but *mamacita* and *papacita*. They promised not to tell a soul they'd ever heard of him.

The day trip would have been as hot aboard an express. They had to leave the windows open to let in a little fresh air and a whole lot of desert dust and engine soot. They'd named the stretch north of El Paso the Journey of Death when you could only cross it on horse or on foot. A steam locomotive crossed it much faster, or might have if it hadn't stopped so often for way-freight.

As it was, Longarm and Jenkins got to talk a lot before sundown, but even after he'd treated the son of a bitch to a fair supper, Dai Jenkins kept insisting he'd never met Professor Powers, Bran Williams, or Rhys Morgan.

When Longarm pointed out they were fellow Welshmen who'd hung out in that same small settlement of Slagtown, Jenkins said with a snicker that he'd been out of touch down Mexico way.

Longarm lit a cheroot for himself alone and told the smirking cuss in a stern fatherly tone, "I can see you figure you're too smart for me by half. So I'll just let you figure out why you want to come clean as the driven snow by the time we get to Denver."

He enjoyed a luxurious drag on his smoke before he added, "We had this first sergeant in my old outfit. Like he used to say to the boys too smart for him, if I can't make you do it, I can make you wish to Christ you had!"

Chapter 13

When they got off the train needing a bath the next day, Dai Jenkins was still insisisting he had no light to shed on the late Professor Powers's postmortem chess moves. So Longarm checked his baggage and marched his prisoner over to the nearby Federal House of Detention. He found they'd rotated old Stubby Sheen to the day watch again.

Stubby Sheen asked the usual dumb questions about how they booked a man arrested in Mexico for a killing in Texas on a federal charge. But Stubby was smart enough to wait until they'd shoved Dai Jenkins in a cell before he asked Longarm privately what in blue blazes they were holding the rascal on.

Stubby said, "Judge Dickerson ordered him released the last time we had him in the back. What'll you bet he gets a writ of habeas corpus on us, seeing he ain't wanted federal?"

Longarm soothed the shorter watch commander with a cheroot, and even lit it for him as he said, "Let's not go picking nits when I'm only out to help the wayward youth, Stubby. I want him held on suspicion, incommunicado, for as long as we can stretch it. We don't have to tell any damn lawyer or the Texas Rangers where he is for . . . what, seventy-two hours?"

"That's pushing it perilously close to unconstitutional," the old hand warned as they stood in the corridor blowing smoke. Longarm nodded, but said, "I ain't out to punish anybody cruel and unusual, Stubby. I might be able to save his neck for him if he sees the damn light before we just have to let Texas have him. You can see how I'm in no position to tell anyone right out loud they have a head start on the Rangers from the front door of this fine establishment. I have to let Dai Jenkins figure that out for his fool self."

Stubby blinked and asked, "Can we do that, knowing he's wanted for a killing by Texas?"

Longarm shrugged and said, "Not if the district attorney of El Paso County or even Judge Dickerson over at the Denver Federal Building has a thing to say about it. But what can anybody say if they don't know I just hauled that boy's ass back from Mexico to save his soul? He killed a man in Texas. He might be able to help us nail nine killers left on that sneaky old killer's list. I figure that's a fair exchange for a running head start before we nail him, or he nails his fool self."

Longarm blew a thoughtful smoke ring and added, "Men who gun other men over false-hearted women ain't on this merry-go-round for the longest possible ride."

Stubby sighed and said, "I wish I had a nickel for every poor young boy I've watched them hang for the love of a wicked woman. I get the point, and you can count on us for seventy-two or a writ, whichever may come first."

Longarm said, "I don't see how anybody but a handful of Mexicans and us could know I cuffed him in Juarez and hauled him way up here so informally. But wonders never cease, and I'd be much obliged if you could hold anybody coming to visit Jenkins for as long as it might take you to get word to me."

Stubby Sheen shook his head sadly but firmly and replied, "I ain't got the authority, and I hope you understand it'll be *your* ass if they ever ask how come we were holding that dear child incommunicado for no more than seventy-two tops."

Longarm must have looked sort of wistful as well. For Stubby added in a helpful tone, "We naturally log all visitors in and out. I can be a mite picky about identification, home addresses, and such."

Longarm said that sounded better than just guessing about visitors who seemed to keep in touch with owlhoot riders by some sort of wireless telegraph.

He asked, "Speaking of visitors who might speak Welsh in the back, do you recall that Miss Glynnis Mathry who attended the hanging of old Professor Powers?"

Stubby thought, shrugged, and said, "Just that one time I saw her out by the gallows with you and that reporter from the *Denver Post*."

"Are you certain she never visited the professor earlier?" Longarm insisted.

The chubby turnkey nodded, then hesitated to consider. "She might have been logged in by old Rhoda, being a female and all."

Longarm frowned and asked, "Rhoda? You mean that head matron with a sweet tooth that sort of shows where she sits?"

Stubby nodded sternly. "Rhoda Bryce, and it ain't from eating more sweets, or more anything else, than most of you skinny folks."

Longarm kicked himself inside his skull and said soothingly, "I never said *you* had a fat ass, Stubby. Even if you had one, we were talking about Glynnis Mathry, remember?"

Stubby said, "Let's go ask Rhoda then. She'd know more than this child about females sneaking saws in to the prisoners. She gets to frisk 'em if they look suspicious to her. Ain't that a waste?"

As they headed into a side corridor toward the front offices, Stubby added, as if Longarm hadn't followed his drift, "I mean, us poor male turnkeys only get to feel up *boys,* while the matrons get to grab at tits and asses."

Longarm didn't think it would be wise to ask about turnkeys of more peculiar persuasions. He'd already insulted fat folks without thinking.

It was just as well he had a firm rein on his tongue when Stubby led him into the cubbyhole of Head Matron Rhoda Bryce. For the poor thing had gained a good ten pounds since last he'd looked close enough to decide she'd be sort of pretty if she could shed enough lard to grease the skids for a battleship launch.

She jumped up from her desk, blushing like a young gal caught in the tub with all her duds off, and asked what she could do for Longarm.

He told her he was there to talk about another gal. Just the thought of old Rhoda doing anything more personal was both silly and awesome to contemplate.

So Longarm told the baby-faced fat gal what he was looking for, and she looked as if she was fixing to cry when she had to confess she'd never laid eyes, or hands, on anyone answering to the description of the petite Glynnis Mathry.

She said, "The only female visitors the poor man had all the time he was here said they were his sister and his daughter. They might have been telling the truth. But they came on separate occasions, and didn't seen to have heard about one another when I asked."

Longarm smiled thinly and said, "That sounds like Professor Powers. What did these two Welsh ladies look like, Miss Rhoda?"

The fat gal replied, "One was a busty blonde and the other was a tall thin redhead, or so she would have had us believe. She must buy her henna rinse wholesale. Both of them were expensively dressed in cheap taste. Why did you just assume they were Welsh?"

Longarm explained, "Everyone else connected with the

104

professor seems to have a Welsh name, and ain't *Bryce* one, as soon as you study on it, no offense?''

Rhoda Bryce looked confused and confessed, "I thought we were Irish. Maybe it's Welsh, if you go back far enough. My grandfather would know. He will go on about some English lord called Strongbow and all those Welsh archers he invaded Ireland with.''

Then she added, "I'd have to dig through old files now that the prisoner is no longer with us. But I think the tall henna-rinse called herself his sister, while the busty blonde said she was his daughter. So they both signed in as Powers, see?''

Longarm nodded and told her, "That would have been less of a chore for either of 'em than making up a whole new fake name.''

She looked as if he'd said something dirty, and asked, "Ooh, do you think I was right in suspecting them of being . . . you know . . . wicked ladies?''

He soberly replied, "Ain't sure they were ladies. Might not have even been his kin. You'd know either one on sight if she came back to visit yet another prisoner, right?''

She said she would, but seemed confused as to why the sister or a daughter of the late Professor Powers would come back at this late date.

She said, "The man lies dead in the morgue even as we speak. I heard nobody has come forward to claim his body. But surely nobody would expect us to be keeping it on ice here!''

Stubby Sheen was the one who explained. "Longarm thinks a new fish in the back may run with the same gang. He wants us to keep a sharp eye out for anybody, male or female, coming to visit one Dai Jenkins. Mainly because nobody but a member of the gang should even be able to make an educated guess that we're holding him, see?''

The far from pleasingly plump young matron dimpled as girlishly as she could manage, and allowed it would be an

105

honor to help the famous Deputy Long track down a gang of female outlaws.

Longarm didn't have time to tell them how he'd fussed at those fool reporters about his ongoing sagas in rival newspapers. He said he had to get on home to wash up and change into duds that didn't make a man look like a fugitive from a coal mine.

They both seemed to want to walk him out the front, as if afraid he'd get lost if he had to find the street entrance by himself.

On the front steps, Stubby said he could count on them, and asked where they could get in touch with him in a hurry.

Longarm said, "Old Henry, the kid as plays the typewriter for us at the Federal Building, can take any messages if I ain't around the office. I have to see about watching the morgue and Lord knows how many other places by the time I'm done."

Rhoda Bryce said, "You won't catch anybody at the morgue, Custis. I was talking to one of their attendants about that when they came by to ask us if anyone had asked about that unclaimed body. He said any kith or kin of a gang leader might know we'd suspect them if they came forward to claim the body."

Longarm sighed and said, "That's likely why nobody's come forward yet. But one reason you don't leave a duck blind early is that a good duck hunter tends to have more patience than the average duck. So I'd like to let Dai Jenkins stew a spell while the professor grows colder, and we shall see what we shall see. I'll come back and compare notes before it's time for all of us to call it a day, hear?"

So they shook all around and parted friendly.

Longarm went back to the depot to get his grimy baggage and tote it home to his furnished digs while he was still grimed and sweaty. Then he wiped his McClellan, saddlebags, and Winchester clean with a change of rags before he took a hot tub bath with two changes of soapy water.

Cleaned up and wearing fresh cottons under his tobacco-tweed three-piece suit again, Longarm reported in to Marshal Vail late enough that afternoon to start planning a pleasant evening with a certain young widow woman up on Capitol Hill. For it seemed a shame to waste all that bay rum on merely filing his field report.

But that Scotch poet had likely met up with a boss like Billy Vail before he wrote his poem about the best-laid plans of mice and men. For old bullet-headed Billy beamed across the cluttered desk at Longarm until he got to the part about letting Dai Jenkins stew overnight in their lockup. Then Billy ruined it all by saying, *"Bueno.* I'll have to forgive your risking another war with Mexico, seeing you got away with your just plain unauthorized arrest in another country of a man you had no federal charges on."

Vail blew an octopus cloud of pungent cigar smoke across a clutter of wires and warrants as he added, "I agree he's likely to sing louder and pay more heed to the lyrics if we give him time to see for himself why he'd rather sing for us than for Texas. Meanwhile, we just got this wire from Fort Smith about a pimp. Seems he tried to recruit a thirteen-year-old ward of the government off the Cherokee reserve for his stable of exotic whores. That's what they call a whore who could be part Indian, part colored, or maybe Chinese—exotic. Judge Parker, over to Fort Smith, got a tip the slimy rascal has his remuda working that arcade down to the south end of Larimer. So, seeing you've been laying around hotels and train stations most of the week . . ."

"Hold on!" Longarm said, "Any junior deputy or, hell, Denver P. D. ought to be able to pick up a pimp who's working his whores at a known location. Meanwhile we still have nine names on that dead professor's list, and the one called Taffy Richards is close at hand, out Aurora way, a short ride east of town."

Vail nodded soberly and said, "If we know that, Professor Powers knew that. So I ain't sending the deputy he might have expected me to send after such a handy cuss. I'm sending that new kid the professor never could have heard about, Deputy Hertz."

Then he added, "Taffy Richards may or may not be laying for *you*, old son. We suspect Richards of a heap more than we can prove. Lord only knows what Professor Powers might have told him you were fixing to pin on him. But he's been living openly in sin with an Arapaho breed out at that Aurora address. So we'll see what we shall see when a sort of stupid-looking salesman shows up on his doorstep with a concealed weapon."

Longarm said, "I follow your drift. The professor was a mighty slick chess master. But no matter how hard he planned ahead, there was no way he could have foreseen you sending me after another crook entirely while a pawn that couldn't have been on his imaginary board heads into a trap meant for me and me alone."

Vail nodded grimly and said, "Damned right. We've taken *one* of his pawns alive, and Hertz ought to be able to capture another in shape to talk. That ought to checkmate the dead bastard, no matter how complicated he was planning ahead when he hit the end of that rope!"

Chapter 14

Visitors from New York City said the Broadway they had in Denver didn't remind them much of the one back home. But most allowed Larimer Street was a worthy rival to New York City's Bowery.

Larimer ran north and south, four blocks east of the Union Station. That was about as far east as the trail herders, yard hands, and such from the the pens and chutes of Butcher Town were welcome, and about as far west as proper folks went unless they had a train to board or some livestock to buy or sell.

The results along Larimer catered to both sorts of customers, with tastes high and low. You had light opera next door to flea circuses, and many a vaudeville house could entertain you with pretty ladies in pink tights on the stage, or gals with nothing on at all, while you sat up in a private box where nobody down in the regular audience seats could see.

The shows got gamier and the music got brassier as you trended south along Larimer. The street crossed Cherry Creek by way of its notorious Larimer Street Bridge, replacing the one that had broken loose in the big flood of the war years to erase a lot of downtown Denver. But although the street continued south into the less fashionable parts, it ended there abruptly as far as most respectable white folks from Denver saw things. Longarm roomed southwest of Cherry Creek. Rents were far lower, and he was big enough to take care of himself where the streets were neither paved nor lit after dark. But it was generally understood by the sporting bloods of Denver that anybody prowling south of the Larimer Street Bridge for cheaper whiskey and duskier whores was on his own.

Hence it had likely struck a new pimp in town as simple supply-and-demand when he commenced to herd his more exotic wares *north* of the tacit line. There were no signs posted, or even city ordinances on paper, Denver having sided with the Union during the war. But just as a Scotch-Irish Texican was supposed to know better than to kiss the bride at a wedding down Mexico way, streetwalkers who weren't exactly white were supposed to know better than to work that arcade north of the Larimer Street Bridge.

Longarm got there well before sundown in spite of taking the time to go to the morgue and House of Detention, because he'd left the office even earlier than he and that young widow woman might have had in mind. The sort of glorified greenhouse covering most of the last block before the creek was as good a place as any to order supper. So Longarm did so, munching hot tamales baked in corn husks and wrapped in newspaper, like the English folks served fish and chips. It was a swell way to eat, standing tall near a back wall of the arcade, with a swell view of the early evening crowd, which was still thin.

He knew streetwalkers of any complexion liked to hit the streets around five, to get set up for misunderstood husbands on their way home from work. So even though the sun still shone through the grimy glass above him, Longarm wasn't surprised to spy old Leadville Lily near the candied-apple stand.

She looked like hell. Many a man and many an opium

110

pipe had been poked in that once-pretty but now piss-yellow and hollow-cheeked face since last he'd admired her up in the high country.

He'd never felt the call to pay for one of Lily's famous French lessons. But he got on tolerably with whores in spite of the fact, or maybe *because* of the fact, that he was more willing to buy the lady a drink than pay for her pussy. So he finished his last hot tamale and wiped his fingers with newsprint as he commenced to ease over to the candied-apple stand.

But a smirking young jasper dressed cow, with his hat crushed Texican style, got there ahead of him to murmur sweet nothings in the sick whore's jaded ear.

To which Leadville Lily coyly replied, loud enough for Longarm to hear yards away, "Don't hand me that shit, cowboy. If it's romance you're after, wait around for some nigger or spic to show up. I just take your money, take care of your dick, and we part friendly, see?"

The horny young cowhand must have. For they left together in what struck Longarm as unseemly haste as he sighed and muttered, "Aw, wasn't that sweet?"

Then he brightened as he saw Leadville Lily had sort of answered the main question he'd meant to ask her. She'd confirmed that tip about "exotic" whores working this end of Larimer. So he glanced up at the glass overhead again, and decided he had time for some cheesecake and black coffee before he'd have just cause to arrest anybody. Billy Vail hadn't sent him over this way to arrest any whores, and even if he had, Longarm didn't see any now that old Leadville Lily had left with her customer.

As he worked his way through the free-standing counters to the booths along the back wall where they sold stuff warm, he spied yet another familiar female coming in from the heavier traffic outside. Rhoda Bryce, the fat matron from the House of Detention, had a silly hat pinned atop her dark upswept hair that utterly failed to go with her uniform dress. But ladies were supposed to wear a hat of

111

some sort in public, and old Rhoda was a lady when you studied on it.

She just wasn't the sort of lady many men *studied* on, bless her lack of visible bone structure.

As their eyes met, the fat gal waved and came lumbering over to tell him Stubby Sheen had told her Longarm might be arresting some wicked gals over here at the arcade.

Longarm's puzzlement must have shown. She added, "I was on my way home from work. But I'd be proud to help you search and cuff any female suspects, lest their lawyers try to compromise you in court."

He started to tell her not to talk silly. But he sensed she'd likely be hurt worse than some, and he'd already stuck his foot in his mouth about fat folks with old Stubby.

And her offer wasn't totally silly. He said, "As a matter of fact, I'm more likely to arrest the federal want they work for. But soiled doves can be a bother when a man's only out to arrest their pimp, and you look like a lawlady who can bulldog bad gals."

"You mean I'm a tub of lard," the fat gal said bitterly, although honestly enough.

Longarm gallantly replied, "Had I meant to call you a tub of lard I'd have called you a tub of lard, Miss Rhoda. I meant you worked at the Federal House of Detention as a professional who could frisk and wrangle female prisoners more delicately than us menfolk. So take that chip off your shoulder if you aim to work with me, and I'll buy you some coffee and cake."

She dimpled, blushed, and said she shouldn't. But he never had to twist her arm to join him at the coffee stand for that rich cheesecake. He noticed she put four spoons of sugar with all that cream in her coffee too.

But she was over twenty-one, and it was good to know her obesity was not a medical condition. He'd already noticed she moved gracefully on her feet, the way a lot of healthy fat folks seemed to, and he'd seen her take a knife away from a gal being brought in one night a year or so back. So as they stood there stuffing their faces, Longarm filled the fat matron in on the plan. She seemed a mite let down when he explained he wasn't after anyone on that dead chess master's list that evening.

He said, "Life must go on, and we have other pawns to play chess with a dead man. Nobody's been by to visit Dai Jenkins or claim the professor's remains at the morgue. So the game might well be over."

She made a little pink asshole with her lips, and asked about all those other names on the list the old sneak had tried to hide in vain.

Longarm said, "To begin with, I figure that list was meant to be found. How else was I supposed to go all the way down to El Paso for Bran Williams, Rhys Morgan, Red Cornell, and Dai Jenkins to ambush me?"

She nodded soberly and said, "Stubby and me were talking about that. The mean old professor told you where to go and then told them you'd be coming!"

Longarm said, "That's about the size of it. I'll never learn to play chess like he could in life. But I play well enough to know you can only plan so many moves ahead because the other player is always going to make some moves of his own, smart or dumb. The professor had two sets of pawns set up in El Paso to cross-fire me. When the Texas Rangers swept Williams and Morgan from the board, Red Cornell had been told I'd likely stay at the same hotel, and then *that* move fell apart when Dai Jenkins refused to play his part in the game. I'm still sort of anxious to hear just what in thunder Professor Powers told those four to get them so riled at me. Another deputy ought to be back from Aurora any minute with yet another name on that fatal list. But what would you care to bet old Taffy Richards wasn't told anything about me good or bad?"

She said, "I remember Taffy Richards. I thought his nickname was sort of silly because he had jet black hair."

Longarm said, "Taffy is an English nickname for a Welshman. It has something to do with a Welsh river called

113

the Taff. The folks who live along the Taff have all sorts of hair.''

He washed down the last of his cheesecake with the last of his black coffee and recited a sort of mean English poem that went:

> *"Taffy was a Welshman,*
> *So Taffy was a thief.*
> *Taffy came to our town,*
> *And stole a side of beef."*

She stared up adoringly and asked how he knew so much about Wales and Welsh folks all of a sudden.

He said, ''Don't tell nobody, but I read in bed. Up until a few days ago I couldn't have told you the Welsh folks were all that different from the English, or that Bryce might be a Welsh family name, no offense. But having Welshmen out to kill you has a wonderous way of concentrating your mind, and once you start to study the subject, it ain't all that tough. It's like studying the Cousin Jacks or Cornish hardrock miners over in the high country. Most regular Americans hardly notice the way those English-speaking Cousin Jacks stick together and shove a mean Irish or Italian boss down a mine shaft now and again. I reckon that's because, like the Welsh, the Cornish fail to strike us as much different from us, next to Italians, Bohemians, Swedes, or even brogued-up Irish.''

She asked if he was making a veiled remark about her own family.

He laughed easily and said, ''You talk and act regular American, and you allowed the name might have started out Welsh. How many times do I have to tell you I come right out with my insults when I set out to insult somebody, Miss Rhoda?''

She sighed, swallowed the last of her over-sweetened coffee, and allowed that others had said she was too sensitive for her own good.

Before Longarm had to come up with an answer, two garishly dressed young things hove into view near the punching bag you got to hit for a penny. So Longarm murmured to the matron, "Yonder, in the rainbow outfits of artificial silk. Wouldn't you say those two qualified as sort of *exotic*?"

The fat gal viewed the two more fortunately proportioned ladies of advanture with ill-concealed disgust as she flatly declared, "Uppity colored hookers. Dressed too flashy to be maids out to pick up some white meat!"

Longarm said, "Look again. You seldom see full-blood Indian gals in high-button shoes, Dolly Varden skirts, and fashionable hats. The federal charges against the man I'm after involved a younger Indian gal. But those two could be off a reservation as wards of the Bureau of Indian Affairs too!"

Rhoda said, "Goody. Let's circle in on them from two sides and arrest them!"

Longarm shook his head and said, "Let's hold our fire and arrest all concerned. If we see either leaving with a gent who can't be made to match our want, we let her serve him and get back to us. If we see one leave alone, after money might have changed hands, we follow her home to her lazy white pimp."

He took the fat gal by one arm and started to move her along the line of stalls as he added, "If we see a tall, thin drink of water with a waxed mustache and a diamond ring, that'll be our want, coming to gather in the sheaves. I'll tell you who to go after then."

She asked, "Where are we going now, Custis?"

He said, "I'm scouting for a duck blind. They've described me a heap in the local newspapers, and you're in uniform, no offense. So I reckon it would be best to let 'em *guess* we were watching those exotic young gals. I suspect we can work in close enough to overhear any criminal conspiracy, if I'm right about the architecture of this glorified greenhouse."

He was. He found a gap between two booths, one shut down and the other manned by a wise old bird who just nodded when Longarm flashed his badge in passing.

Behind the lined-up booths there ran a narrow gap between the temporary wood and canvas and the solid bricks of the arcade's back wall. There was plenty of room for Longarm's hips. But poor Rhoda had to crab sideways. Then, as he'd planned in the beginning, they came to a booth near the punching bag the two whores were using as their own base of operations.

The booth was not in use. It stood as a musty empty shell behind its pulled-down canvas front, ready to offer any goods or service a renter might have in mind.

Since nobody was renting it, Longarm pried loose a couple of back boards and helped Rhoda inside. She needed a little help.

But once they were in there together, grinning like apple-stealing kids in the dim light, the fat gal giggled and whispered, "Ooh, I feel so naughty in here where nobody in the world can see us! I mean, we could be doing all sorts of wicked things in here and that crowd out front would never know!"

Longarm gulped and said, "I better cut a peephole so we can see what *they're* up to out front."

Chapter 15

The two Cherokee gals didn't seem to be up to much when Longarm poked his pocket knife through the painted canvas for a better look. He knew they were Cherokee because they were murmuring to one another in that lingo. Longarm didn't speak enough Cherokee to matter, but he could tell they weren't talking Osage, Creek, or the other Muskeegan dialects you heard over near Fort Smith. There was a certain ring to each lingo, and so he'd guessed Cherokee even before he picked up on a few words he knew. One was likely talking about nearby Cherry Creek when she mentioned a *chika*. All streams and rivers with a *chika*, such as Chickamauqa or Chickahominy, had been named by some Cherokee in olden times, Chika Mauga meaning River of Death while Chika Hominy translated roughly as Corn River.

On the far side of the runaway Cherokee, Longarm spotted old Leadville Lily, back already from her alley romance with that cowboy. When he chuckled dryly, Rhoda Bryce asked him what was going on and what he found so amusing.

He whispered, "Keep it down. I'm tolerable sure we're

watching the gals our want recruited off the BIA. But they ain't doing nothing yet. I had to chuckle because a white gal in the same line of work just got back from a mighty short stroll down the primrose path.''

The fat girl pouted. "I'll never understand you silly boys paying for what's there for the asking if only you knew who to ask!"

To which Longarm could only reply, "Some old boys can't take it when the object of their desires calls them a pathetic critter. I ain't in the habit of hiring hookers, if that's what you're asking."

She whispered back, sort of dirty, "So we've been given to understand, you naughty boy! What's the full story about you and that dumb blonde from the stenographers pool at the Federal Building? The one they call Bubbles?"

Longarm felt his ears burning as he replied in a desperately calm tone, "Miss Bubbles ain't that dumb. She spells swell, and who told you there'd been anything betwixt us fellow federal employees, ma'am?"

The hefty matron answered flatly, "*She* did, at a meeting us girls held about equal pay for equal hours. She bragged that you'd shown her the best time she could remember on that leather chesterfield in that judge's chambers."

"Did you gals get your pay raises sorted out?" Longarm dryly asked. "Or was talking dirty all you managed at your secret meeting?"

Rhoda sighed and replied, "They told us we were free to quit if we weren't happy working for the government. Bubbles didn't get up and make a speech about the many times you made her so happy about working for the government. Just a few of us were talking over coffee and cake after the meeting broke up."

Longarm managed not to mutter that he'd thought old Bubbles might be indulging in too many snacks since first he'd helped her out of that corset. But it wasn't easy. Gals who kissed and told were just as bad as boasting Don Juans, if not worse. Hardly anybody ever believed a *man* when he

118

cackled about getting laid for free by some famous actress. But let a female confess she'd been to bed with a famous actor or, hell, the president of these United States, and everyone figured she had to be confessing instead of bragging.

An older gent who looked like a church deacon was talking to one of those Indian whores now. He looked old enough to be her granddad, and likely was. You could tell he'd negotiated with many a whore in his time by the calm expression on his lived-in face. He knew he had what they wanted, and if they weren't willing to give it to him at the price he was willing to pay, he knew that old Leadville Lily, watching wistfully from up by that candied-apple stand, would likely service him way cheaper.

Rhoda sounded as if she was having trouble breathing as he whispered a running account of the goings-on out front. When the dirty old man lit out with not one but *both* naughty Cherokee, Longarm sighed and said, "That does it for a spell. No way a man half his age could enjoy what two gals have to offer in less than the better part of an hour. But I ain't sure we ought to break cover, lest that pimp I'm after comes by to see how they're making out."

Rhoda agreed they were better off standing pat, even though it was sort of stuffy in there. As she opened her uniform bodice, she bulged even more than he'd expected, murmuring, "I'm trying to picture what one man could do with two women at the same time. I can't come up with anything that doesn't sound awfully depraved!"

To which Longarm could only reply, "That's likely why he wanted to hire the two of 'em, Miss Rhoda. He looked like a married man to me."

"You mean married to some poor frigid thing who's unwilling to be a good sport in private where nobody else can see," the fat matron stated rhetorically as Longarm warned his fool groin not to tingle like that.

It wasn't that he felt too proud. Her face wasn't bad and her big ass promised a whole lot of novelty. But they worked for the same old Uncle Sam, and if she'd heard about him and Bubbles, Bubbles and the other gals in the stenographers pool were sure to hear how far he'd managed to shove it into all that quivering lard.

As if she'd read his mind, fat Rhoda moved closer to husk in his ear, "I'd never tell. I've been crazy about you for years. But I'll bet you never heard it from anybody else, Custis!"

That was the simple truth. So he gulped and quietly asked her who else she might have told about this undeserved honor.

She sobbed that she'd been holding it in and holding it in, until the next thing he knew she was holding him by the crotch of his pants as she put her other big strong arm around him to haul him hard against her big soft tits while she pleaded, "Don't laugh at me, Custis. I know I'm making an utter fool of myself, but please don't laugh just yet."

He kissed her lest she spy the shit-eating grin on his lips, and it didn't feel as grotesque as he'd expected. For as that kindly old philosopher had written about cats in the dark, a gal felt a lot like a gal once you got to feeling her at all. Although it wasn't at all true that they all felt the same, Lord love 'em. For try as he might, Longarm just couldn't recall anybody with tits like this one's kissing him so sweet and girlish while hauling his cock and balls out through the fly she'd just unbuttoned so skillfully.

So he didn't fight her as she hoisted her uniform skirt just as deftly. Taking advantage of a moonstruck fat virgin would be one thing, while common courtesy to an obviously desperate pal would be another thing entirely.

He could tell how desperate she was when she got her skirts up even with his gunbelt to guide his throbbing erection where she'd removed any underwear she might have started out with. Both partners had to know what they were doing when they did it standing tall against the back wall of a frame booth. So he had no call to ask delicate questions about precautions when she raised one fat thigh to hook the arch of a high-button on the counter behind him and just reached out with the thick wet lips of her old ring-dang-doo to literally suck him up inside her, hissing, "Ooh, is all that meant for just little old me?"

He cautioned, "Keep it down! Your voice, I mean. There's somebody out front, and I agree we ought to keep this our little secret!"

So they did. But it wasn't easy, with old Rhoda moaning that she wanted him to do her *right*. Naked in bed, over to her place, with his lovely manhood probing her inner being to the very depths. Gals who daydreamed a lot about a gent before they got to screw him tended to talk that way.

He promised to come on home with her later, being human and about to come in her surprisingly tempting two hundred pounds or so. Then they somehow wound up on the duckboard flooring, with her on top, his pants half down, and her playing stoop-tag atop him, despite all that weight that she had to bounce up and down.

It looked shocking and felt swell. By the time she'd come and sort of sucked him off with her quivering innards as she pressed all that titty-lard against his chest, he meant it when he said he couldn't wait to bang her bare-ass, dog-style, with the lamp lit.

But as sanity slowly returned, they both became more aware of the male voices muttering quietly just out front. For all of a sudden, with no warning, a slice of light pierced the gloom above them as a somebody pried the front canvas open long enough for a glance inside, then let it pop back in place, muttering, *"Nid oes dim neb yma."* Somehow Longarm could tell by the tone that he and old Rhoda hadn't been spotted below the level of the front counter.

Just as he somehow knew they couldn't be speaking Spanish, French, or Cherokee when another voice said, soberly, *"Na ato Duw. Yr oedddwn i yn gwydbod."*

Longarm rolled the owl-eyed Rhoda off him—it wasn't easy to do that silently—and hauled up his pants as he whispered, "Be still and stay down. There's no federal statute forbidding it, but them gents out front are jawing about something or somebody in Welsh!''

As if to prove his point, one of them banged casually against the booth, making both folks inside suck in some breath, as he went on in English. ''This empty booth would make a fine sniper's nest, look you.''

His companion hissed, *"Yn Gymraeg!"*

But the one less comfortable in Welsh snorted, *"Paham?* Who might be close enough to overhear us in this crowd? *Saesneg* ears perk up when they overhear the distant lilt of The Valley. Why don't we duck inside this empty booth and speak all we wish, more privately, in any *iaith,* look you?''

So Longarm crouched over the quivering fat gal on the duckboards as he quietly drew his .44-40, whispering, ''They're moving off. But you just heard 'em talk about hiding in here with us.''

She gasped, ''Oh, Lord, they're moving around to come in the same way we did!''

To which Longarm soberly replied, ''I just said that. I want you to stay put until I tell you to move, or until you don't think I can! Dive out the front and run like hell if it looks like I'm losing.''

Then he kissed her on the brow, rose to his full considerable height, and eased out into the dark slot behind the lined-up booths.

He saw he'd done so just in time.

The two sons of bitches lined up for his one gun in the narrow slot saw the fix all three of them were in at about the same time. The one nearest Longarm at point-blank pistol range was the only one of them in shape to throw down at short notice, gasping, *"Iesu Grist, ei fod yma!"* as he raised the muzzle of his own drawn six-gun an instant too late.

Longarm, being braced for the showdown, fired first, and kept firing as the narrow space filled with billowing gun smoke and total confusion, what with gunshots echoing, fat gals screaming, and at least one bullet spanging off the back bricks to banshee-wail its way down the dark narrow slot.

Then it got as quiet as could be while Longarm hunkered low to reload and strained his ears in the clearing gun smoke. He could tell fat Rhoda had taken his advice about diving out the front when he heard her yelling at somebody else out in the arcade while police whistles chirped in the distance.

It was almost dark outside, with just a sickly funereal light coming down through the overhead glass as Longarm eased in on the two figures he'd laid low in the narrow space. He could tell they both lay dead. A man got to where he could tell, after his first war. But Longarm still had to hunker over each in turn to make certain.

The trouble with standing right behind a man catching two-hundred-grain slugs with his hide was that most of those slugs were still moving fast enough to kill you once they'd finished killing *him*. Longarm just knew they were going to raise a fuss at the coroner's hearing when his official report said he'd put those ten holes through two men with the five rounds he'd been packing in the wheel. That one ricochet he'd heard had doubtless passed through both bodies before hitting the bricks and bouncing. Bullets came out most any old way if they clipped a bone on their way through a cuss.

Neither total stranger was wearing Welsh folk costume. Both could have passed for plain old American country boys, dressed for rough riding. Longarm couldn't say yet which had been wearing his hat high-crowned with a Texas crease, and which dimpled cavalry-style. The one who'd been closer had been armed with a Colt '74. The other had a Schofield .45, still holstered. That army model was more likely to go with a cavalry hat, though Longarm wasn't ready to take either of the sneaky rascals at face value just yet.

A male voice called his name, and Longarm called back, ''Back here behind the booths!'' knowing good old Rhoda had been talking about him out front. But he still covered the slot with his six-gun until, sure enough, a copper badge wearing Denver P. D. blue ducked through that narrow entrance down the way.

By this time Longarm was searching the bodies for their wallets. So when the copper badge joined him, he was able to say, "I somehow doubt these old boys were named Olsen and Bergman. They were plotting to ambush me in Welsh."

The copper badge hunkered down beside him and declared, "I can't say I recall either of these boys on my beat. But we heard about you federal lawmen being after that gang of Welshmen, Longarm. Your Deputy Hertz just had a swell fight with another specimen of the species out Aurora way. The meat wagon was dropping the results off at the morgue less than an hour ago."

Longarm gasped, "Jesus H. Christ! They killed young Hertz?"

To which the copper badge cheerfully replied, "Not so anyone would notice. The way I heard it, Deputy Hertz got the drop on this Taffy Richards cuss and offered him the chance to come along with or without the cuffs, subject to his good behavior."

Longarm grumbled, "Damn it, we warned the kid Richards might be dangerous. What happened?"

The copper badge said, "Richards made a break for it as they were mounting up out front. They say your Deputy Hertz made a fine shot at a moving target. Old Richards was likely dead before he hit the ground."

Longarm stared down at the bodies sprawled between them as he sighed, "That makes three more we can likely scratch off our list, once we can figure out who these two were and how in thunder they knew where I'd be looking for another want entirely."

He added morosely, "Neither me nor my boss could have known where I'd be headed this evening. So how in blue blazes could that sneaky Welsh wizard have known before they hung him?"

Chapter 16

Rhoda Bryce thought she knew. There'd been no honest way to get out of some promises made in a moment of pleasure. So once things were sorted out at the south end of Larimer Street, Longarm had to take the fat gal home to her place above a carriage house on Lincoln.

Trying to be a good sport, Longarm managed to get inspired some more by thinking of the alarmingly skinny Leadville Lily while he sort of wallowed in the naked fat of the heaving and moaning Rhoda.

Her notion of doing it naked with the lamp lit had not done a thing for Longarm's remaining passion. Picturing another figure with his eyes closed helped. Old Rhoda marveled that she'd never had a man that deep in her before. He believed her. Getting a gal that hefty to spread her legs wide enough took considerable effort no matter how long or short the rest of a man might be. So it was just as well he'd read that translated Hindu book about lovemaking, with illustrations.

Rhoda moaned in pleasure when she wasn't laughing dirty about him living up to all she'd heard about his bad habits in a lady's bedroom. There was no polite way to tell her to shut up and let him come. But by the time he was ready to, he decided old Rhoda was likely tighter and certainly cleaner down yonder than that disgustingly skinny Leadville Lily. So he managed to mean it when he pounded them both to glory in a manner to make her glad they were alone in the carriage house that evening.

It was after they'd come unstuck to just cuddle and share one of his cheroots when Rhoda decided the dead professor was getting some help on this side of the morgue.

She said, "I've been thinking and thinking, honey dong, and it's just not possible for anybody to think that far ahead. That mean old chess master may have sent warnings to his pals that you were coming, then left that list so you'd go. But there was no way he could have pictured you invading Mexico, or staking out that arcade to arrest a want nobody in Denver knew about at the time of his hanging."

Longarm placed the smoke to her rosy lips and agreed. "Those last two weren't waiting for me there. They were sent. I thought it possible, but stretching the art of prediction, when Red Cornell and that dying Mex were sent to that hotel I didn't really have to go to. If Jesus Gomez is still alive down yonder, he knows less about Professor Powers than Dai Jenkins, and Jenkins keeps insisting he hadn't heard a thing about any Professor Powers."

She passed the smoke back and cuddled her considerable charms closer as she stated without asking, "But you've established Jenkins as a pal of that Red Cornell the professor sent after you at that hotel."

There was something to be said for pillow conversations with a gal who rode herd on crooks for a living. He patted her plump shoulder and said, "Jenkins never said he didn't know Cornell. He said Cornell had invited him to come along and kill me because another, ah, business associate had warned Cornell I was in El Paso to arrest the both of them."

She puffed too hard on the cheroot, coughed, and said, "Wait a minute, lover. You had no federal warrant on ei-

126

ther of those bad boys. Shouldn't they have known that?"

Longarm took a drag on the smoke and replied, "Nobody in the gang but the late Professor Powers himself was reputed to be such a deep thinker. When your average slow-witted quick-draw man gets a tip from a pal he trusts, he acts on it. Hired toughs who've studied law books are by definition too smart to call hired toughs."

He blew a thoughtful smoke ring at the low ceiling above her brass bedstead and mused aloud, "How and why might a deranged economics teacher recruit at least thirteen plain old hardcases? What did they all have in common, for Pete's sake?"

She said, "Well, they all seem to be Welshmen, or at least Americans who speak some Welsh."

He shook his head and said, "That only adds up to half the picture. Crooks of the same background tend to trust one another more than crooks from another. But crooks gang up to do something crooked. Nobody would recruit a gang of Chinese hatchet men just to ambush lawmen. That Irish bunch that organized as the Molly Maguires back East were out to scare the mine owners into paying them off, not to sit around and sing lots of Irish songs. So what would a financial genius and confidence man do with thirteen Welsh gunslicks of limited brains or even table manners?"

The obese prison matron commenced to fondle his sated shaft for him as she suggested, "You're going at it backwards. Come to think of it, that's one way we haven't tried. Roll me over and mount me doggy-style while we talk about other naughty girls."

He was surprised he was still able to get it up. But thanks to a little help from a mighty skilled friend, he could. So it was amusing to stand there beside the bed, a lit cheroot gripped between his teeth, as he grinned down at the awesome ass she was thrusting up at him while she knelt on hands and knees across the mattress.

As he parted her big fat buttocks with his palms to plumb

the depths between with his old organ-grinder, he casually asked her who they might be talking about.

She arched her spine and replied, "Ooh, nice! Keep doing it just like so! I was talking about that wicked Welsh girl who stole your original list from you. Did you do her *this* way, you brute?"

Longarm didn't think it would be wise to allow he had, only deeper, thanks to the petite brunette's far smaller ass. So inspired by the memory, he thrust hard into Rhoda's big rump and replied, "For Pete's sake, she done me dirt, honey lamb! But who told you about her running off with those thirteen names and addresses? I don't recall us talking about her until just now."

Rhoda explained, "Oh, we've all been talking about the case over at the House of Detention. We all knew Professor Powers, and of course you have that snotty Dai Jenkins over in the male wing now. I forget just who told me that brazen brunette followed you halfway down to El Paso aboard a night train unchaperoned. I think it was Stubby who suggested she could be planning to use that list he found for her own sinister purposes. Could you move just a little faster, huggy bunny?"

He did so absently as he thought back to another gal entirely. Just what in blue blazes could old Glynnis have wanted with that list of names? Reporter Crawford of the *Denver Post* had told Longarm she was a published writer. But Longarm couldn't recall ever reading anything by any Glynnis Mathry, and he spent lots of time at the Denver Public Library when he was low on money on a rainy Saturday afternoon. So he made a mental note to scout their index files the first chance he had.

Out loud he decided, "I'll ask around. But I'll be mighty surprised if she's still in town after stealing official papers off a federal lawman."

Rhoda grunted, "Faster! Don't stop! That bitch could wire anybody on that list from anywhere in the country, saying she was old Professor Powers and ordering them to

128

gun a man she was sore at. Why might she be sore at you, lover? Did you pull it out of her at a time like this?''

Longarm groped for her hipbones under all that padding, got a good grip, and administered some good old-fashioned barnyard rutting as one small sane part of his mind considered *how* rather than why the most pissed-off brunette in these United States could have known he'd be patrolling for pimps at that arcade around sundown. There was no way the pretty little thing could be watching him that tightly unless she was still in town. So he sort of came in Glynnis and Rhoda at the same time as he sincerely hoped nobody at all had watched him walk this sweet-screwing tub of lard home!

It made him feel two-faced and dirty, as swell as it felt, to be taking advantage of a good old gal he'd be ashamed to be seen with in public. He remembered that Justice Department hoedown they'd held last Thanksgiving Day, and how dumb he'd felt dancing a few go-rounds with old Rhoda, because he'd had to, with her staring up at him so adoringly and that ash blonde over by the refreshment stand teasing him about his conquest.

He'd meant it when he'd told the far more temping ash blonde there was no way he and old Rhoda would ever wind up more than fellow federal employees. But here he was coming in her, and Lord have mercy when she bragged about it to that same ash blonde over at the House of Detention.

As they lay panting side by side some more, he asked Rhoda if she wanted him to light another smoke. She said she'd had enough. He thought she meant tobacco until she added, ''Custis, we have to talk. I'd be a big fibber if I said I didn't want you to stay the night and screw me silly for breakfast. But these other girls will be coming by to walk back to work with me in the morning and . . .''

''Say no more,'' he told her, kissing her big tit sincerely as he sat up to add, ''I have a landlady who just don't understand a roomer who might want to entertain an overnight guest. So what say I just go fold my tent like that Arab and slip silent into the night?''

She murmured, ''You're not hurt? I don't want to hurt you, Custis. It's just that I worked so hard to get promoted to a senior matron, and I'd hate to have them talking about me at work as a fallen woman.''

He assured her gallantly, ''You ain't fallen no farther than a heap of us, Miss Rhoda. Anyone can see you're only blessed with a warm and generous nature.''

She said she didn't want anyone to see, and made him promise he'd never brag to anyone they knew about her begging for it on her hands and knees, for heaven's sake!

He assured her he wouldn't even brag about kissing her. So she said in that case he could kiss her some more because it was still early and she wanted all the loving he could give her to remember him by.

Longarm took her considerable charms in his strong bare arms and kissed her good, French-style, before he asked in a desperately casual way if they were talking about just one fast screwing.

She sighed and said, ''I'm afraid things have to be that way, poor baby. I know you want to keep screwing me. I'd love to keep screwing you too. But we work together, and it would never work out if we kept meeting like this. I'll never forget this one night of love for as long as I live, but we have to be discreet. Nobody else must know, and you know there's no way two people who meet like this after work can hide their feelings. There's something about the way people look one another in the eye, after they've seen one another naked.''

He said he followed her drift and kissed her some more, feeling great about the way things were panning out. She seemed to take his friendly kissing for passion, or at least she acted like she did, when she grabbed him by another dawning erection. He couldn't help wondering how often she might have played this sad renouncing scene with other

130

actors. But fair was fair, and he'd only wanted to try her on for size. So what the hell.

As their petting grew more passionate, Rhoda said she was sure glad he was willing to settle for this one sweet session, and she got him to repeat his promise that he'd never tell a soul he'd been up there.

Once he had, she coyly confessed that, seeing they meant to part friendly and agree none of this had ever happened, there were just a few teeny-weeny things she'd always been curious about.

He soberly accepted her tale about having read about those naughty French notions in this book she'd come across by accident. But once she had her rosebud lips puckered tightly around his turgid shaft, he knew damned well she'd played *that* coy scene before. Because nobody had ever blown the French horn that melodiously without a lot of both instruction and practice!

Longarm had no improvements to suggest as he just lay back to let her call the tune. He'd have felt some distaste for her Little Miss Innocence act if it hadn't felt so good, and what the hell, he'd been making believe about his own feeling towards her, the way most folks did at such times.

He chuckled fondly, and started to comment on how moon, June, and honeymoon were just polite words for fucking and sucking once you got down to bedrock. But he never did. He knew she enjoyed her secret sex life better when she thought she was fooling her victims.

He wondered just how many victims the poor lonesome fat gal had had by now. She was no spring chicken, and anyone could see, or feel, she'd had one hell of a lot of experience.

He groaned, "Don't make me come this way, honey. I want to finish in you right!"

So she let him, and from the Mona Lisa smile on her round moon face as he pounded her hard as if she'd been pretty, he suspected she'd had just such a pounding in mind when she'd worked it up for him some more with that much skill.

Later, she fell asleep in his arms, or pretended to. She failed to wake up, or chose not to, as Longarm disentangled from her big soft curves, rolled out of bed to wash up at a corner stand, and silently slipped into his duds and strapped on his gun as he was easing downstairs in the dark.

Out on Lincoln Street he consulted his pocket watch under a lamppost and declared, "Well, I'll be switched with snakes! Did we do all that before midnight?"

Then he headed west along the deserted residential streets, crossed Broadway, strode toward the south end of Larimer by way of more than one shortcut, and doubled back before he paused in a dark alley to study his back-trail, assuring a tomcat watching him from atop a trash can, "Ain't nobody following me. Anybody who just spied me leaving that carriage house would expect me to head for home at this hour. So let's just mosey over to that arcade and see if any sons of bitches are still out to stop me from carrying out the chore old Billy Vail gave me to begin with on this mighty unusual evening!"

Chapter 17

The cheaper hangouts along Larimer got more crowded as the night wore on and fancier places closed down. So the arcade had come back to life, and then some, when Longarm strode into the gaslit cigar smoke and cheap perfume around midnight.

Peering through the crowd for someone to talk to, he spied Leadville Lily over by the tamale stand, looking desperate as well as desperately sick while she seemed to be feeding on the smell of all those steaming hot tamales.

They cost two for a nickel, and an ugly whore with an opium addiction had to budget her appetites some.

Longarm moseyed over to nod at the fat Mexican who sold the snacks and tell him, "Wrap us two servings, Pancho. I'm hoping Miss Lily here will do me the honor of dining with me this evening. You better give us some of that hot chocolate too. It's getting sort of brisk since the sun went down behind the Front Range."

Leadville Lily blinked up at him and croaked, "Custis Long, you old basser! Have you come back to shoot this place up some more? Things are just getting back to natural. And how did you know I missed supper earlier?"

Longarm replied soberly, "It's a gift, Miss Lily. I don't want to fornicate with you again, but I'm fixing to feed you and then give you your going price before we say anything else."

The once-pretty whore stared up owl-eyed as she asked, "Again? Did you ever? It's hard to keep track, but up Leadville way, I had the distinct impression you only paid us girls for information."

Longarm watched Pancho tong tamales out of his steam chest and wrap them in cones of newsprint as he told her, "I was only teasing my ownself, Miss Lily. Before you lie to me, I'd best explain I ain't been demoted to the pimp patrol. The federal want I'm after ain't wanted in Fort Smith for pimping. They want him for dealing in stolen goods. That's what they call it when you steal wards of the government off a reservation and peddle their exotic flesh in another state."

As Pancho handed Lily her order, the hungry whore allowed she had a good notion who they were talking about. But she dove in without a word more.

Longarm accepted his own tamales and hot chocolate more politely as he continued. "They call him Candy Pants Collins. I got the names of the Indian gals here somewhere, but they're likely calling their fool selves something like Fifi or Yvette on the street. Suffice it to say, two of 'em are Cherokee and one's Muskeegee or Creek."

Leadville Lily just washed down a heroic mouthful of hot tamales with hot chocolate. It was Pancho who said, "They come through here a lot. They were in here earlier. But only two of them are Indian. The younger one is a *Negra*. Not bad-looking but, *Madre de Dios,* she has a *boca cagado*."

Longarm got down a more delicate bite and asked, "Who was this mysterious colored kid insulting, Pancho?"

The older man said flatly, "Everybody and everything. She has been spoiled by all the attention from gringo customers. So nothing is good enough for her around here.

134

She even called my tamales dog shit. I am sorry, Señorita Lily, but that is what she said I made them out of. She said where she came from tamales were called bat mammas and tasted ten times better.''

Longarm brightened and asked, ''Are you sure she didn't call those tamales *batnahas,* Pancho?''

The Mexican looked relieved, and declared, ''That is the word she used. How did you know?''

Longarm said, ''I been sent over to the old Indian Nation a time or more on other business. I've eaten *batnahas,* and she was right about them tasting different.''

He regarded the tamales in his big fist thoughtfully as he explained. ''Tamales in general were invented by Indian cooks somewhere in olden times. So the names and recipes vary some. These here Mexican tamales are the old Aztec version, from name to peppered stuffing. *Batnahas* are a Muskeegee version, made out of the same cornmeal and steamed in the the same corn husks, with a different stuffing entirely.''

He enjoyed another bite and added, ''I find this version way more interesting. They don't use chili peppers over to that Creek reserve. But I can see how a gal raised on blander *batnahas* stuffed with a sort of gray-green mush might find your hot tamales a scary surprise.''

He sipped some hot chocolate, nodded, and decided, ''Lots of folks listed by the BIA as Creek Indian look sort of colored to the rest of us. When they were fighting us from creek to creek in the Old South, the Muskeegee took in a lot of runaway slaves. That Black Warrior River in Alabam' ain't named after any regular-looking Indian. So that fresh-mouthed young gal and the two older Cherokee add up to the BIA stock that Candy Pants Collins stole.''

He turned soberly to Leadville Lily and asked, ''Where can I find him, Miss Lily?''

She looked as if she was fixing to cry as she told him, ''I can't tell you. You have those three girls down pat, and I have heard them call him Candy on occasion. But you

135

have to understand. Those three damned breeds ain't work-ing this arcade because us white girls *admire* them.''

Longarm nodded gravely and said, ''I'd ask you to tell me the name of the fixer who calls the tune in this police precinct, but you'd tell me where to find Candy Pants Col-lins before you'd tell me that.''

It had been a statement rather than a question. But Lead-ville Lily felt obliged to plead, ''Don't go away mad, Cus-tis. You've always been nice to me and I'd do most anything else you asked, in or out of bed.''

He smiled thinly and replied, ''I know. A gal just has to draw the line somewhere.''

He knew the tamale-stand man was willing to talk but didn't know much, just as he knew what might happen to a streetwalker who talked *too* much. He also didn't want anyone listening in to hear him say they'd already told him enough. So he just finished his snack, put the used mug back on Pancho's tray, and allowed it had been nice talking to them.

As he turned away Leadville Lily followed, plucking shyly at his sleeve and murmuring, ''Custis, you, ah, said something about giving me some money?''

Longarm stopped, turned to her under a gas jet, where the cruel light really made her look desperate, and fished out a couple of coins to hand her as he said, ''I'm sorry, Miss Lily. I forgot. I don't reckon there's anything I could say that would get you off that dream-pipe, is there?''

She sobbed, ''If there was, do you still think I'd be smoking the shit? I'm sorry too, Custis. Sorry about a lot of things, and right now, sorry I just can't help you more.''

He allowed they'd already settled that, ticked his hat brim to her, and turned to stride out into the night as the wretched Leadville Lily fought back the impulse to run after him.

She didn't. There were things you just didn't do on the street if you wanted to go on living, and as vile as life could feel away from her opium pipe, Leadville Lily wasn't ready to experience death.

Longarm got his bearings outside, cut through a service alley, and found his way to a hole-in-the-wall saloon on Wazee Street. At that hour there were only a few regulars leaning against the bar. Longarm stode past them toward the back rooms. The redheaded barkeep called out, "You can't go back there, mister."

To which Longarm modestly replied, "Sure I can. I carry a badge, and if that ain't enough, I pack a double derringer and a .44-40."

So nobody tried to stop him as he twisted the knob of the back-room door, found it locked, and stepped back one pace to kick the door off its hinges.

As the busted door crashed in at them, the five men seated around a poker table reacted in various startled ways, but nobody was about to draw when they saw the one and original Longarm looming in the now-doorless doorway and smiling wolfishly.

Nodding at a squat Black Irish type in a pug hat and side whiskers, Longarm said gently but firmly, "I'd like a word in private with you, Knuckles."

So Knuckles O'Hanlon, the fixer of that precinct, told the rest of his boyos to beat it, which they did with quiet efficiency.

As soon as they were alone, O'Hanlon smiled up at Longarm like a mean little kid and said, "Alone at last and you with me undivided attention, me darling. Do you want to tell me who gets on top, or was it something else you wanted to me to do for you?"

Longarm said, "I think you're beautiful too. But it's getting late and my patience is wearing thin. So before you bullshit me and I have to bust anything else around here, I'd better repeat what I'd heard about you warning the low-lifes you protect not to bust any federal laws."

Knuckles O'Hanlon sighed and said, "Aroo, and that's the simple truth of the matter. For the precinct captain costs

137

me enough, and there is no way I could be after buying that stuffy President Hayes, and him not allowed to drink under his own roof, sweet Jasus!''

Longarm placed a boot on the seat of a vacated chair and leaned on that knee with an elbow as he said, ''I'm sure glad we see things the same way, Knuckles. I'm after your new boy in town, Candy Pants Collins. I'm packing a federal warrant on him, signed by Hanging Judge Parker of the Fort Smith District Court. It seems he removed some names from the Indian Allotment Rolls without asking permission and—''

''Say no more,'' Knuckles O'Hanlon cut in, taking out a business card and stub pencil as he added, ''The fix we agreed to made no mention of federal raps. So I'll be writing down the street number of the rooming house they've been staying at, over on the other side of the creek.''

He scribbled swiftly, and rose to hand the card across the table to Longarm as he asked in a desperately jovial tone if they could still be lovers.

Longarm pocketed the card, allowing what Denver P.D. had to say in the matter of local vice was a local matter. But they didn't shake, and neither felt really friendly as they parted wary but polite.

Longarm crossed Cherry Creek by way of the Blake Street Bridge, and found Candy Pants Collins alone in his quarters, getting dressed to go out, as he kicked in yet another door.

The tall and big-boned but oddly soft-looking pimp let out a sort of girlish gasp and started to go for the Starr .32 in his shoulder holster before he thought better of it.

Longarm beamed at the oily bastard, his own gun still holstered, as he said softly, ''Go for it! *Please!*''

But Candy Pants Collins pasted a salesman's smile across his pale face and answered almost smugly, ''No, thanks. One of the few things my dear old daddy left me, along with an empty bottle of rum, was some sage advice on gunfighting. So, to what may I owe this late visit, friend?

I can see by the fact that I'm still alive that you weren't sent to kill me in cold blood."

Longarm said, "I surely wish I could, you baby-raping pussy-monger. But as you've likely surmised, I am the law. Federal. So now I want you to put on that coat, turn around, and let me cuff your wrists for a late-night stroll to the lockup."

Candy Pants asked what the charge was. Longarm told him to just do as he was told unless he wanted to ride to the damned lockup on a damned stretcher instead. So a few minutes later they were on their way, and it only took a few more to leg it back across the creek to the Federal House of Detention.

Once there, they found the night shift had rotated to another head turnkey Longarm knew, an older gent they called Pop Wetzel. As they were signing the Indian thief in, Longarm asked Pop if he could borrow Dai Jenkins for a spell.

Pop Wetzel asked, "At this hour? There's hardly anything open in town this late, old son."

Longarm started to explain. He decided not to. He said, "No offense, Pop, but lately I keep finding mean Welshmen laying for me everywhere I go. We call it the process of eliminating when we scratch suspects off our list because they just couldn't have done it."

Pop Wetzel said he hadn't known he was on anybody's damned list, and that Longarm was welcome to sneak off to anywhere he had in mind with that sneaky Welsh boy.

So a few minutes later, now pushing two A.M., Longarm and a bleary-eyed Dai Jenkins were legging it along a deserted side street, Jenkins cuffed to Longarm's left wrist by his own right as he protested, "Not so fast. I'm still half asleep, and where on earth are we going?"

Longarm swung his prisoner into a dark doorway, glanced back the way they'd just come, and answered pleasantly enough, "Denver Morgue. Got a couple of other Welshmen I want to show you."

As they moved on Jenkins protested, "I'm as American as you are, damn it. It was my elders who came from Cardiff. I rode for the Union during the war, durn it."

Longarm said, "No, you didn't. You forget we've got the story of your miserable life on your considerable criminal record. You sure are one devious rascal, Dai. Don't you never tell the damn truth?"

Jenkins insisted he never lied. So Longarm wasn't surprised, a few minutes later, when their prisoner stood in the cool cellar of the morgue like butter wouldn't melt in his mouth, swearing he'd never laid eyes on the late Professor Powers, the backshot Taffy Richards, or those two more recent arrivals from the gunfight at that arcade.

Longarm thanked the morgue attendants, and gruffly led Jenkins back outside. When Jenkins asked where they were headed next, Longarm growled, "Back to your cell. Then I mean to wire them Texas Rangers to come and fetch you, you fool secretive simp! If you'd just as soon hang as talk, I reckon you and Texas deserve one another!"

But this was not to be. For as they got about a block and a half from the morgue, with Jenkins protesting a mile a minute that he'd be proud to talk if only he had anything to say, a shot rang out in the darkness behind them, and a second shot might have taken Longarm right between the shoulder blades if the dead man cuffed to his left wrist hadn't pulled him down to the sandstone pavement.

Then Longarm had his own gun out and trained back the way they'd just come, as he hunkered above the sprawled body of Dai Jenkins.

But he saw nothing, and all he heard was the faint, fading sound of running footsteps. For the son of a bitch had just killed his prisoner and run off like a thief in the night!

Chapter 18

A backshooter who could scurry one way in the dark could just as easily scurry another way. So Longarm had uncuffed himself from the corpse of Dai Jenkins and taken cover in another dark doorway by the time he heard a police whistle chirping his way from the other direction.

He called out, "Over this way! I'm the law too! But watch out for other sons of bitches waving guns around here! I know for a fact one of 'em ran north around the corner!"

A blue-clad roundsman hove into view with a bull's-eye lantern. As he swung its wan beam on the bleeding face-down cadaver of Dai Jenkins, Longarm warned, "Keep it trained that way, or better yet, put it out! We *know* where we are. Let the other side *guess*!"

The young copper badge doused his light as he dogtrotted over to join Longarm in the doorway, asking, "Who's that poor soul they shot so dead, Longarm?"

Seeing there was no need to introduce himself, Longarm told his fellow lawman, "Suspect name of Jenkins. I just now had him visiting some other suspects at the morgue. I'm still working on whether they were aiming at him to

shut him up, or me because he might have already told me
more than they wanted me to hear.''

The copper badge glanced out across the walk at the still
form of an annoyingly silent rascal in life as he opined, ''I
heard two shots. Sounded to me as if they were out to do
you both in.''

Longarm nodded soberly and replied, ''I noticed. The
only thing I got over 'em now is that they just don't know
how much I know.''

They heard more whistles, and saw another bull's-eye
lantern beaming their way. The copper badge with Longarm
hailed his pals in, and then all four of them, lanterns beaming ahead of their gun muzzles, made certain they had the
deserted business district to themselves save for the one
dead crook.

Some night watchmen and night-prowling drunks beat
the meat wagon from the morgue to the scene. Longarm
was repeating his tale to a late-arriving detective with a
drinking problem when they were joined by Reporter Crawford from the *Denver Post*. He said he'd been covering a
fight in a whore house when somebody had said something
about a backshooting over this way.

Longarm had mixed feelings about the burly cuss in the
checked suit and derby. Crawford was a good old boy. He
had this habit of turning a dropped jar of olives into a
wagonload of watermelons demolished by a train. But there
were times it might pay to advertise, so Longarm said he'd
fill Crawford in on the fly if he cared to tag along.

Crawford allowed he would, but begged Longarm to
slow down as they legged it back toward the House of
Detention. Longarm said he had some chores to tend to,
and suggested Crawford just squat down and piss like a
woman if he couldn't cover ground like a man.

Crawford called him a hard-ass, and complained that
he'd been promised a damned story. So Longarm brought
him up to date on his eventful evening, leaving out all the
gals he'd fooled with along the way because none of them

142

worked as suspects and he was afraid the *Denver Post* might say he was engaged to one or more of them on its social page. But then, as he edited old Rhoda, Leadville Lily, and those Indian Agency runaways out of the story, the story began to make more sense.

He said, "Bless you, my child. Billy Vail calls what I'm doing a process of eliminating, and let's talk about a female suspect I *haven't* been able to eliminate. Do you know where that Glynnis Mathry who went to that hanging with you went afterwards?"

Gasping for breath, or maybe pissed off, Crawford replied without a trace of warmth, "Sure, I know where she went after she ducked me at the hanging I thought we were covering together. She went with *you*! Downtown Denver is my beat, and more than one of my street tipsters saw her board that night train to El Paso with you."

Longarm replied, "Don't get your bowels in an uproar. She ducked out with that list of names Professor Powers had been trying to swap for his neck. I was hoping you might know why, or where in blue blazes anybody could sell such purloined paper."

Crawford said Glynnis had never returned to Denver as far as anyone he knew could tell. He asked Longarm to elaborate more on those names the gal with two pretty faces had run off with. Longarm told him just enough to make sure he'd run the story in the *Post*. When Crawford asked how a dead man could be setting up ambush after ambush from the Great Beyond, Longarm replied in a worried tone that he found it mighty spooky himself. The less the other side knew the better, and he wanted Crawford to report that the law was buying an impossible story.

It had only been a few short days since all this spooky bullshit had commenced, and it was already starting to look certain that a live confederate of the late Professor Powers was moving his pawns around the board for him.

As they approached the gloomy mass of the federal lockup, Reporter Crawford showed he really could think sensibly, in spite of the Wild West tales he was inclined to write about his pals. He suggested that since the flirty travel-book writer who'd run off with her own copy of the list had been Welsh-American, she might well have been kith or kin to a high-toned crook.

Longarm grunted, "If she's at all well-known as a writer, she won't be too tough to track down. We're still working on that tall blonde and short redhead who claimed to be the old crook's sister and daughter. In the meantime, I have this other chore to wrap up. So here we are, and it's been nice talking to you."

The puffing sweaty bastard strode right up the steps and into the damned lockup with him. A lot of crack reporters were like that.

Pop Wetzel had already heard about the shooting over by the morgue, since news traveled faster than a participant wrapping up a police report. But Pop took the loss of a prisoner like a sport, seeing Longarm had signed Jenkins out and it wasn't his own ass sticking out.

Longarm said in that case he'd have a word with the prisoner he'd brought in earlier, and told Reporter Crawford flatly that he couldn't listen in.

So he got to talk to Candy Pants Collins alone in the back, for all the good it did him. The pimp had been given time to simmer alone in a patent cell. But he was an old hand at the game, and Longarm found him stretched out on the bunk, jerking off to while away the wee small hours.

Longarm stared morosely through the bars and muttered, "Cut that out. You ain't got enough there to show off with it. I want to talk to you about your whores. I can see why they were anxious to go out on the street to get laid."

Candy Pants let go of his organ-grinder, which was actually massive, and swung his feet to the floor to grin up at Longarm slyly and remark, "A lot *you* know, and I'm proud of my tongue as well. I don't know nothing about no whores. I'm too pretty to pay for it. Did somebody tell you I've been picking up whores? Is that what this is all about?''

Longarm fished out a smoke for himself alone, not feeling he owned the bastard shit, as he patiently said, ''You're going back to Fort Smith, with or without those reservation runaways. Do you really want Judge Parker and their tribal councils to suspect you abused them worse than anyone suspected?''

The well-endowed pimp snorted, ''You'd play hell proving I've ever abused any of my . . . girlfriends. I don't have to. They call me Candy Pants because of the powers of persuasion I was endowed with by good old Mother Nature. It ain't just a matter of size, you understand. A man has to know what he's doing with it when he meets a bored housewife or ambitious hotel maid.''

Longarm finished lighting his cheroot and insisted, ''I ain't got federal jurisdiction over white gals who run off with you. We were talking about two Cherokee and a Muskeegee.''

''Were we?'' asked the worldly pussy-monger. ''I reckon I'll stand pat and see what my lawyer wants me to say. Ain't no way to extradite me to Arkansas from Colorado without letting me have my day in court.''

Longarm almost said something dumb. But you never wanted to tell a crook how dumb he was. So he blew smoke at the bastard and moseyed out front again to find Pop Wetzel alone at his desk again.

Longarm said, ''Make sure nobody tells Collins we don't need to hold an extradition hearing on a federal charge. I'll tell him after I take some more wind out of his sails. I'd like a word with the matron in command of the woman's wing tonight, if it's jake with you.''

Pop Wetzel got to his feet, saying, ''What the ladies have to say about gentlemen callers is up to them. Fat Rhoda ain't on duty at this hour, though.''

Longarm's lips felt sort of numb as he managed to sound calm while asking the sly old dog to clarify that sly remark.

Pop said in a less-strained way, "I figured she was just bragging. But you may as well know you have more than one staff female lusting after your fair white body, old son. Female prisoners talk, and you do spend a certain amount of time here, where it sure can get dull and the staff is inclined to talk about the only subject most of the human race is really interested in."

Longarm thought back to the deal he and Rhoda Bryce had just made naked in bed. He decided it was safe to say, "I've never bragged on kissing nobody, before or after I've kissed 'em."

Pop said, "The rest of us thought she was just dreaming. More than one of the better-built matrons has allowed you surely never made eyes at *them*!"

They entered the head matron's cubbyhole, where Longarm was mildly surprised to find that ash blonde from the department hoedown on duty.

He was glad. He knew that if old Rhoda went back on their deal to crow about his weak nature here at work, it would be a matter of female record that he'd been on duty, with his pants on, during the night in question.

But all he told her was that he aimed to arrest some gals, and wanted some other gals to back his play and bear witness that arrest had been all he'd had in mind.

So forty-five minutes later Longarm was back up in the quarters of Candy Pants Collins and his exotic gals, with a couple of more ordinary gals wearing uniform dresses and U.S. Army-issue Schofield .45 Shorts. One of the junior matrons was a perky little gal with an unfortunate face. The other resembled somebody's pretty grandmother.

They couldn't talk, holed up in the dark inside an occupied rooming house. He'd given them their instructions out back by the shithouse, and told the landlady downstairs what would happen if she or that one boarder who'd stuck a head out as he was arresting that pimp earlier sent word to wards the U.S. Government really wanted back.

So the three of them had much more time to kill in si-

lence than most folks would have been able to kill without
fidgeting. One window faced east, and the sky was just
starting to pearl lighter over that way when they heard
somebody open the backyard gate.

Longarm snapped out of the wet daydream he'd been
allowing himself with a well-built ugly gal, a pretty old
lady, and fat Rhoda.

He didn't have to say anything to the gals he'd just been
enjoying in some shocking positions. They had ears as well.
So they were both flat against the wall, guns drawn, on
either side of the open doorway as Longarm stepped out in
the hall and crawfished back in the darkness at the head of
the stairs.

He heard the other gals murmuring back and forth in
Cherokee as they came up the stairs. When one of them
giggled dirty, he wondered idly whether that old man
they'd gone off with had ever tried *three* gals at once. Then
they were on the landing with him, and sure enough, one
of them noticed the way he'd kicked their door in earlier,
and said so urgently!

But of course as they turned to bolt, Longarm grabbed
an arm with either fist as the two matrons poured out into
the hall to help him subdue and cuff the two of them.

They were still cussing him in Cherokee when he and
the matrons herded them back into their quarters and lit a
table lamp. He'd sort of forgotten how young they looked
until the lamplight revealed the tears of rage and fear cours-
ing down their powdered tawny cheeks.

He said, "Simmer down, ladies, while I tell you how
this story has to end. As soon as that Muskeegee gal you
all ran off with comes back from *her* last sporting propo-
sition, we're taking the three of you over to the women's
wing of our Denver lockup. If you behave like sensible
prisoners, you'll be treated like sensible prisoners. If you
keep cussing and spitting like that, you'll likely consume a
heap of bread and water before Fort Smith gets somebody
out this way to take you home."

One of them said a dreadful thing in English about his mother. So the motherly matron hit her.

Longarm said, "Don't do that no more, Miss Kate. We were all young once. I'm sure these sweet young things are going to sit quiet in the dark with us as we await the dawn, or that Muskeegee gal, whichever."

The slightly older of the two Cherokee gals laughed bitterly and said, "Nastassiya ain't coming back here. You'll never catch her!"

The other gal hissed at her in Cherokee. But she shrugged, fixed Longarm with a defiant smile, and said, "I don't care who knows it. She got away. You may have *us*. You'll never catch Nastassiya Nittakechi! She don't have to walk the streets no more, see?"

Longarm got out his notebook and asked her to spell that Muskeegee name. She told him to go fuck himself. The matron hit her again. But Longarm said, "Never mind. I see I already wrote it down off that Fort Smith warrant. These other ladies would be Hazel Tenkiller and Susan Bluefeather of the Civilized Cherokee Nation. That's what you call an Indian gal who streetwalks in a city, civilized."

He put his notes away and demanded, "What's the story? Did she get a job in a house of ill repute, or has some rich customer set her up as his own private stock?"

The talkative one started to answer. Her sister in sin kicked her, and she told Longarm to fuck himself again.

He just chuckled fondly, seeing she'd answered that question for him with the look of pure envy in her big sloe eyes.

He told the other gals, "Let's herd 'em on home. There's only so many places in or about this town a man could keep a pretty Indian gal who looks colored. So like the old song goes, farther along we'll know more about it."

Chapter 19

Longarm was used to going as long as seventy-two hours without sleep if things were interesting. But even after a hot shave and a cold shower, he was yawning some as he brought Billy Vail and Henry up to date at the Federal Building later that morning.

Old Billy Vail had been a lawman longer than Longarm, and could track across dusty-filed papers better than your average Paiute could track rabbit across snow. So he was the one who said, "Let *us* worry about all those unaccounted-for females. I don't want my deputies getting laid on the taxpayers' time."

The pallid Henry said, "If this Glynnis Mathry is who she claims she is, it shouldn't take more than a day or so to locate her publisher or publishers, and legal residence."

Vail growled, "Damn it, Henry, I just said that. A colored-looking gal installed somewhere as the spoiled play-pretty of some rich moon-calf ought to cost us no more than the sort of legwork I can assign Smiley and Dutch or, hell, young Deputy Hertz."

Henry asked how he knew they were talking about some rich lover. Vail looked as if he was fixing to explode. So

149

Longarm explained in a more gentle tone, "The gal's an enthusiastic young whore, Henry. A love-struck stockyard worker couldn't afford what she'd demand to be his and his alone. I have it on good authority she's pretty, petulant, and demanding. The sport keeping her is going to have his hands full. She won't settle for any little shack or, come to study on it, a nice place in the colored quarter southwest of Cherry Creek. She considers herself an Indian too good for any Indian reservation."

Vail grumbled, "I just said I'd have that Fort Smith warrant tidied up for you, damn it. Let's get back to that seriously spooky bunch of Welshmen. There's just no way Professor Powers could have foreseen a man he wanted killed taking a prisoner to view his dead body in the wee small hours. Your turn."

Longarm shrugged and said, "The chess master asked one of his pawns to take over after he was gone. If we can catch crooks off guard by just watching for 'em, where is it engraved on granite that they might not have somebody watching the House of Detention or, hell, the front and side doors of this very Federal Building?"

Vail repressed a shudder and said, "Makes more sense than getting instructions from a dead man. Who do you reckon they were out to kill last night, you or their captured pal Jenkins?"

Longarm shrugged again and said, "They fired twice. They might have helped Jenkins escape if that first round had hit me instead of him. On the other hand, they might have aimed to shut him up. *We* knew the son of a bitch wouldn't tell us anything. On the other hand, it was only a matter of time before he sang for us or swung in Texas."

Vail said, "In any event, we know somebody, singular or plural, has been out to pay you back for arresting the old con man before he could slicker them banks and . . . Hold on now. I hadn't thought of that!"

Longarm sighed and said, "I had. Some Mex pals talked to those Mex bankers and wired me nothing we can use.

Meanwhile, none of our own bank officials I've talked to have been able to come up with anything more complicated than a big bank robbery. The first few swindles Professor Powers pulled when he first went wrong involved razzle-dazzle check-kiting betwixt accounts at separate banks. He had opened modest accounts at that El Paso bank and another down in Ciudad Juarez. But recruiting all those dumb but dishonest gun waddies would have made no sense if he was up to his usual flimflams.''

He tried not to yawn again as he said, ''I'd rather *ask* somebody who knows than just sit here speculating with my eyes half shut. I got one name on the list that might be worth looking into. The professor listed a Dilwyn Glass as a rider off the Triple Z, up by Jimtown. I know that neck of the woods. I'd like to ride up that way and see what a man with such a Welsh name might have to say in plain English.''

Vail told him his notion made sense, but not to tell another soul in town where he was going. So Longarm went back to his furnished digs to change into his range denims and get his saddle, Winchester, and possibles.

But just as he was coming down the steps all ready to ride, Henry dismounted out front to declare, ''Thank heavens you hadn't left already. The boss says you don't want to ride up into the high country after all.''

Longarm said, ''Sure, I do. That's where Dilwyn Glass has been working when he ain't holding folks up at gunpoint, according to Professor Powers.''

Henry said, ''Not anymore. He's dead. You killed him. They just sent word from the morgue. A couple of gals read about the shooting in the morning papers and came forward, weeping and wailing. Dilwyn Glass was one of the gunslicks you shot it out with at that arcade last night. The other was call Jack Affon. They were both in town with their women when they got a message written in Welsh. Neither gal can read Welsh, and of course the rascals never left it to be found when they tore out to ambush

151

you, leaving their doxies stranded in a cheap hotel. Marshal Vail's sent for 'em, if you want to talk to 'em back at the office.''

Longarm started to agree. Then he said, "Billy can question suspects better than anybody I know. So seeing I was about to catch a hack out to the Diamond K and borrow me some trail ponies anyways, I reckon I ought to just go ahead and do that."

Henry blinked and asked, "Where might you be riding, seeing Glass and Affon don't work up around Jimtown any more?"

Longarm said, "After somebody else, of course. Tell Billy I ought to be back in a day or so, with or without more mysterious Welshmen."

So they shook on it and parted friendly, leaving Longarm free to catch a ride out to the Diamond K just south of town and have his pal, the boss wrangler, fix him up with a paint mare and bay gelding he'd ridden before.

He made it west to the first hogbacks of the Front Range foothills a little after noon, where he followed a draw he knew for a ways, and then rode up atop a rise to stare all around like a big-ass bird in the sky. He could make out individual rooftops and chimney tops of Denver off to his northeast. A sunflower windmill was pumping water for the only homestead close enough to matter, just to the southeast. There was nothing moving along the trail he'd just ridden west of the South Platte flood plains. He hadn't expected to see anything. He nodded thoughtfully at the faint haze of trail dust settling behind a grassy rise a country mile behind him. Then he turned as if satisfied and rode on.

He repeated what he'd done three more times. Then he dismounted in a more brushy draw at slightly higher altitude to tether his two ponies and build a modest coffee fire on a sandy patch. He chose dry windfall with care, knowing an experienced rider would be expected to. Then he ran like hell up through some aspen and on over a grassy rise to flop down behind some soap weed with his Winchester, removing his Stetson so just his smaller head could peer back the way he'd just come through the yucca-like clumps to both sides of him.

Time slowed down to a crawl again. Somebody had once written that anyone who wanted to live forever might try spending more time in dentists' offices or waiting for trains late at night. A man belly-down in dry cheat long enough for the grasshoppers to start landing on his gun barrel had a lot of time to think with.

Then, after Longarm had given up more than once, but forced himself to wait just ten more minutes more than once, a figure on foot seemed to be coming down the far slope, his own Winchester trained down into the draw as he scouted that rising wood smoke. Longarm could see by his outfit that he was dressed for town or country in a tinhorn suit, but had stout boots and and a large hat creased Texas-style.

He was good, whoever he was. He moved in just close enough to see there was nobody hunkered between that fire and those pony rumps. Then he was crawfishing backwards up the slope, peering all about for the rider he'd been trailing.

So Longarm fired and let the cuss see he had the range, but the harmless geyser of dust to his right didn't seem to inspire the stranger to freeze at all when Longarm called out for him to do so.

"I mean it!" Longarm yelled as the distant figure fired his own Winchester at the smoke of Longarm's first round. Then, as the man turned to run, Longarm fired from his new position, aiming low to take the cuss alive, and had to laugh when he saw what a silly fall a man could take with a bullet in one leg.

As his target rolled back down the slope, screaming that he was mortally wounded and didn't want to fight any more, Longarm broke cover to call back, "Just lay there, clear of that carbine, with your hands polite, you son of a

153

bitch. I'm coming over now, and whether you wind up in the hospital or the morgue will be depend on your common sense!''

The man he'd just crippled yelled, ''I aim to sue you for this! You got no call to gun me! I never done nothing to you!''

Longarm didn't waste his breath at that distance with remarks to the effect that the sneaky rascal hadn't had time to carry out his orders. But it seemed clear enough that you didn't sneak in on a man's last known location with a Winchester when you were out to sell him a Webster's Dictionary.

Crossing the draw and heading up the far slope, Longarm called out not unkindly, ''I aim to tell the court I shot you before you actually busted any federal statutes. As a wounded material witness you may well walk free, once you can walk again. It all depends on how fine a witness you'd care to be, savvy?''

''I'm hurting bad!'' his target wailed. ''Get me to a doc and I'll tell you all I know!''

But then a puff of gun smoke blossomed against the skyline above, and that Texas hat flew away from its owner's head with a lot of his shattered skull and brains!

Longarm snapped a return shot at the unseen killer's gun smoke and crabbed to one side, but kept running up the slope bold as brass because there was no other way he could hope to make the top in time.

As he chose a clump or rabbit bush along the top of the rise to dive into and roll through, he saw another man running down the far slope just as fast as his chunky legs could carry him. He was making for the two chestnut ponies tethered in the bottom of that draw. Longarm fired and shouted, ''Halt, Goddamn it! I won't say that again!''

He meant it. The panic-stricken killer must not have cared. He just kept running until Longarm's second round, aimed low, took him smack in the small of the back and sent him sliding on his belly for some dusty distance.

154

• Longarm muttered, "Shit, I don't even talk Welsh and they *still* keep dying on me!"

He moved down the slope, reloading his Winchester's tube magazine as he did so. Those ponies beyond the fallen figure looked like livery mounts. A pair of retired cavalry steeds with cheap matching saddles.

As he hunkered down over the last one he'd shot to go through some pockets, he muttered, "Somebody watching saw me leaving town. You two figured you'd never have a better crack at me than out here in the open range. You figured wrong. But those two livery mounts ought to be easy enough to backtrack to where you hired 'em."

He found a .36 Navy Colt Conversion and a wallet inside the dusty frock coat. He doubted the man he'd just shot could possibly be Judge Dickerson of the Denver District Court. But that explained the time old Judge Dickerson had hunted high and low for the billfold he'd left in his chambers with his street coat.

Staring down at the dusty dead face of the obvious crook, Longarm said, "We figured this was stolen by some courthouse regular, a cuss who knew the layout of the building, court proceedings, and such. So now we have a dead confidence man tied in some way with border toughs, hired guns, and courthouse sneak thieves with a really mean streak. I don't know about you. But I find this mighty confounding."

He was still trying to make sense of it as he fetched the men's own livery mounts to lift first the short one on the north slope and then the taller on the south slope into their hired saddles.

The second one reminded him of somebody he'd seen before. As he led the two livery mounts down to where he'd tethered his own ponies off the Diamond K, he decided, "That makes sense. No way they could have been watching me all this time without my even catching a glimpse of one nosy face."

He kicked what was left of his decoy fire out, grinding

the coals into the soft sand with a boot heel as he told the two corpses they'd be on their way in a minute.

Then he made sure they were secured with leather saddle strings, improvised a longer trail-line from spare rope aboard his pack pony, and mounted the paint to get on the road at an easy trot. They didn't have far to go, and it was all downhill. He figured he'd hang on to the cow ponies while he deposited the dead meat at the morgue, and then lead the livery mounts to as many downtown livery stables as it might take.

He figured he'd start near the stockyards and work east towards downtown. There weren't any decent livery stables near his hired digs. So anybody watching his place and seeing him leave as if to do some serious riding would have had to scurry back across the Larimer Street Bridge to . . . right, hire those old army brutes at some stable down the creek a piece.

He slowed to a walk to light a cheroot, now that he knew where he was going. Calling cheerfully back to his silent and face-down riding companions, he declared, "I'm starting to back-trail you boys pretty good. You saw me catch that ride south. You knew I'd likely borrow my own riding stock off my pals at the Diamond K and . . ."

How would a college professor gone wrong and a gang of scattered Welsh pals know so much about him and his personal habits?

He blew smoke out both nostrils and decided, "At least *one* of you had to be a Denver boy who's been watching me longer than any out-of-town Welsh wizards, whether he was out to gun me or not."

Then he decided, "Well, of course my Denver pal was only hired to kill me recently. He'd have tried to gun me earlier if he'd been ordered to earlier and . . . Son of a bitch, you boys have sure made a sucker out of me. For I've been playing chess with a dead man when all the time the game was only checkers!"

Chapter 20

Both bodies were commencing to stiffen a bit by the time Longarm got them to the Denver Morgue. But the attendants managed to lay them out flat as one cheerfully told Longarm business had sure picked up since that Welsh wizard had put some sort of Druid curse on him.

Longarm regarded the two stiffs he'd just brought in off the open range and growled, "Ain't sure they were sicced on me by any Druids, dead or alive. One was packing the wallet of a federal judge. The other would have had us believe he was a Methodist minister who's likely missing a wallet as well."

"You mean they were pickpockets?" asked the other morgue man.

Longarm shook his head and said, "I doubt it. Men who live by the gun live by the gun. They likely bought some paper to show in place of their own from some lowlife they knew from the streets of the more sporting parts of town. I'm fairly sure I've seen that one who shot his pal for me somewhere around that Larimer Street arcade."

"Then they were the ones who scouted you for the ones we have on ice from that earlier shootout at the arcade, right?'' asked the one who seemed to know everything.

Longarm said, "Wrong. I'll know better once we find out who these jaspers really were. But when you can't get different pieces of the puzzle to fit, no matter how you try, it's a fair bet they just don't go together. I've been trying to fit these two in with the two last night at that arcade, and there's just no sensible fit!''

He had better luck at a livery stable near the Larimer Street Bridge. They not only wanted their horses and saddles back, but told Longarm they'd been hired out earlier that same day to a Reverend Masterson and a Judge Dickerson, with no deposit, since both gents were regular customers.

Longarm told the old coot in charge he'd have to do better than that if he wanted his damned horses back.

The gray balding hostler smiled up at him uncertainly and bitched, "Them's our ponies and we can prove it. We got bills of sale as go with their brands and our initials are burnt into the back leather of both cantles!''

Longarm grimly replied, "I ain't disputing ownership. I'm talking about material evidence. I have two dead bodies to find names for, and they were both last seen alive aboard these very broncs. So I reckon I'll just lead them over to the government corrals and see if anybody comes forward who might know more about the matter, hear?''

The hostler said, "They were better known amid the sporting crowd as Tex and Utah. I honest to God don't know their real last names. Tex said he worked as a poke over to the stockyards. Maybe he did and mayhaps he didn't. The two of them kept odd hours for gents with any sort of regular jobs. I mean, you'd see them at night and you'd see them at two in the afternoon, and sometimes they'd go riding and other times they'd just be spitting and whittling on the city hall steps, like they were waiting for somebody to hire them for the day.''

Longarm told him his tale was worth the two livery mounts, and rode over to the Federal Building with his borrowed cow ponies. He tethered them out front, and went upstairs to report his latest gunplay to old Billy Vail. Young Henry was interested enough to follow him back to the marshal's inner office.

When Longarm had finished, as tersely as he could manage, the room was filled with even more tobacco smoke, but that wasn't what inspired Billy Vail to say he just couldn't see any sensible pattern.

Longarm raised a polite hand to cover a yawn and wearily replied, "I'm too sleepy-eyed to make hide or hair of the latest beef future quotations in the papers. It might make more sense after I've caught me just a few winks and a heap of black coffee. But try as I might, I can't see who in blue blazes could be predicting where I'm headed before I head there. I mean, I've told one suspect this and another suspect that, but I ain't even told the two of *you* where I was headed every time!"

Henry snorted, "I confess. I've always hated you since you screwed the bubbly blonde from the stenographers pool. So I've been asking all my Welsh pals to lay for you in odd corners. You didn't know I was a secret Welshman, did you?"

Billy Vail told the kid he wasn't funny. But Longarm brightened in spite of his heavy eyelids and said, "You may have something, pard. We do have a heap of names on file out front, and some of them have to be Welsh names. What say the next time you have nothing better to do, you run me up a list instead of jacking off in the shithouse?"

Henry said, "I'd rather jack off in the shithouse. Have you any notion how many names we have in just our current files? After that, I wouldn't know a Welsh name from a regular American name if it jumped out of the file drawer and bit me."

Longarm insisted, "I'm pretty sure Deputy Dewey would be able to help you with that chore, Henry. Dewey is a Welsh name, and I've noticed folks with names like Jones and Jenkins are more apt to be more knowing of such matters than their neighbors like the Smiths or Millers."

Billy Vail took a thoughtful drag on his stinky cigar and told the clerk, "Do it. I knew a Welshman named Smith one time. But Dewey is pulling court duty just down the hall, and ought to be proud to devote his noon break to the cause of justice."

He turned back to Longarm to say, "We've wired Fort Smith about old Candy Pants and those three runaway reservation wards. They'll have a deputy and matron on the way west by now."

Longarm frowned and said, "I wish you'd talked to me about that first, no offense. I wanted to sweat Candy Pants Collins a spell. We have those two Cherokee gals on ice with him, but we're still missing that young Muskeegee, Miss Nastassiya—or Nasty, as she'd be better known along Larimer Street."

Vail shrugged and said, "We got three birds in the hand and the one in the bush can't get far. Call her Muskeegee or call her Creek and she still looks like a pretty colored gal. If she's anywhere in Colorado, she has to peer out through the lace curtains sooner or later, and Fort Smith can just come back for her."

Henry asked, "What if she's hiding out in the colored quarter?"

Longarm and his boss exchanged glances. Longarm explained to the kid, "She, or the prosperous white dude who wants her all for his own, would be spotted even sooner if he set her up in a colored neighborhood. Folks might not gossip to the copper badges on their beat about one of their own. But a sassy reservation gal being kept by a rich white dude?"

Henry tried, "All right, what if he took her out to his country spread, where no neighbors might notice?"

Billy Vail said, "You ain't lived in the country much, Henry. When William Bent lived in sin with Yellow Woman of the Cheyenne Nation on the banks of the Arkansas River, we heard the gossip clean up here in Denver.

If you ever aim to screw your pig or any other species of pet, make sure you do it in a fair-sized *town*. Nobody pays more mind to your habits, good or bad, than country neighbors.''

Longarm yawned again and said, ''Might be worth wiring an all-points want on the missing gal, though. Henry might not be the only one who thinks you can hide a dusky play-pretty out at a homestead or in some smaller town. Make sure you tell 'em she looks more colored than Indian, though. Local lawmen alerted to watch out for an Indian runaway could overlook a scandalous relationship with a colored gal easy.''

Vail grudgingly said he'd do it, and suggested Longarm go home and get some sleep before he passed out on the rug.

Longarm yawned some more and said, ''Got to run two borrowed ponies back out to the Diamond K first.''

Vail said, ''Then do it and go straight home, damn it. You're in no shape for another gunfight, half asleep on your feet. I want you to promise you'll hole up behind a locked door and catch at least one good night's sleep before you go prowling after wild women or Welsh wizards again.''

Longarm got to his feet with another yawn and said he had just the place in mind, where nobody who could be after him would think to come after him.

Vail said, ''Stay away from that young widow woman who lives down Sherman from me and my old woman. If the scandal about the two of you has spread as far as *my* back fence, there's no saying who *else* in the Mile High City might have heard.''

Longarm protested, ''Hell, I'd never put any gal at risk that way, knowing for certain now I've been marked for death by some son of a bitch with a personal hard-on for me.''

Vail said, ''*Bueno*. You have my permit to report in late as usual in the morning. Lord willing and they don't kill you tonight.''

Henry followed Longarm out as far as the front office, saying he'd scout up Deputy Dewey and see how many Welsh names they had on file. So Longarm said, "Let's start with the personnel files. You do have copies of most every Justice Department hand's application papers, don't you?"

Henry said, "No, but I can get them from down the hall if I have to. Why do I have to? Are you suggesting the late Professor Powers had a confederate working for *us*?"

Longarm yawned and said, "Henry, I'm too tired to suggest shit! I just want all the pieces of the puzzle I can gather together for when and if I wake up."

Henry insisted, "How could any turncoat in our department watch you that close if they wanted to?"

To which Longarm could only reply, "Damn it, Henry, if I knew who kept setting me up to be backshot, I'd be able to ask him, her, or it how come! You just heard me say there's nobody at all working anywhere who could have set up each and every ambush in the few past days! I was only half joking when I said I'd even considered you and the boss. That process of eliminating he keeps preaching seem to eliminate each and every soul I've talked to since they hung that fool professor!"

They split up out in the hallway. Henry went to rustle up Deputy Dewey, and Longarm went down the marble stairs and out a side entrance to swap saddles and head back out to the Diamond K aboard the gelding, with the jaded paint mare trailing.

They got out to the Diamond K as the shadows were starting to get longer in the dust, and he was naturally invited to stay and sup on all the sourdough bisquits and salt pork he was up to. So he allowed he'd be proud to. But he waited until after supper, when the hands were mostly smoking out back as they watched the sun go down, before he approached his pal, the ramrod, to explain his delicate predicament.

The laconic grizzled gent in charge was able to think on

162

his feet and make up his mind quickly, which was the main reason he was in charge of all that stock and property. So he just grabbed Longarm by one arm and led him out the far side of the grub hall toward the big house.

Along the way he explained, "The boss and his family are off to that big state fair in Omaha. I don't expect 'em back for a week or more. So you can bunk in the master bedroom, and nobody but me and the household help will ever know you spent the night here, see?"

Longarm said, "I don't know, pard. I'd sure feel silly if I woke up with the boss and his old woman getting into bed with me!"

The ramrod laughed and said, "They'd feel funny too. But it ain't going to happen."

And he was right. It didn't. The only person he woke up in bed with after a good night's sleep was Lolita, the young Mexican housemaid who'd come in to serve him his breakfast in bed and allowed she might as well *keep* serving him, seeing nobody would ever know and she'd never been invited into that fancy bedstead before.

Longarm was too polite to ask her where she usually shucked her duds as fast as she could have peeled a banana. He was just as experienced. Although he wasn't too used to enjoying ham and eggs, jelly on toast, and a blow job at the same time.

He suspected he knew what had gotten into the sassy little housemaid, aside from him, when she got on top all a-giggle. It was fun to screw a gal on the monogrammed sheets of her boss lady, watching them doing it in the fancy dressing mirror, while considering what one might do or say if the boss lady walked in on an uninvited guest *en flagrante* with her household help. He'd heard the kitchen help spat in the gravy at the Tabor Mansion too. The imposing Augusta Tabor ate with a tiara on her head ever since they'd struck pay-dirt up Leadville way.

Lolita took his hurry to finish as a compliment, and came some more so he could take it out and be on his damned way with the sun all the way up, for Gawd's sake.

He forgave Lolita for slowing him down when his leaving without a shave resulted in his catching a buckboard ride into town with a delivery hand. Billy Vail had said it would be all right to report in a little late. So he had the hand drop him off at his own quarters with his saddle, Winchester, and possibles.

Stowing the McClellan and cleaning the fired saddle gun first, he got cleaned up, shaved, and changed into the sissy outfit they expected him to wear on duty in town. Then, packing just his derringer and side arm, he moseyed afoot across town to the Federal Building, arriving a little after ten A.M.

He entered the office with a clear conscience and a friendly smile. But Henry looked up from his typing and gasped, "Where have you been all this time? Marshal Vail's had me hunting high and low for you all morning!"

Longarm said, "Don't get your bowels in an uproar. You found me. What's all the fuss about?"

Henry said, "The last act of *Hamlet*! They found Nastassiya Nittakechi the day before yesterday, on a sandbar thirty miles down the South Platte, stark naked with her skull caved in. They thought she was some dead colored gal until they got our message."

Longarm whistled and said, "Maybe Billy can see how her killing ties in with all this other bullshit. I'll be damned if *I* can!"

As he started back to see Vail, Henry said, "He's not in his office. He went over to investigate that other murder on Lincoln Street."

A big gray cat swished its bush tail inside Longarm's guts as he numbly asked, "A murder on Lincoln Street too?"

Henry said, "I said it was getting messy. Rhoda Bryce, that matron over at the House of Detention, never reported for work this morning. She didn't have as understanding a boss as we have. So they sent somebody to see what was keeping her. They found her stark naked too, facedown on her kitchen floor with one side of *her* skull caved in!''

As Longarm spun on one heel to light out, Henry added, ''You just got a wire from El Paso too. That Mex you shot down yonder, the one called Jesus Gomez, died last night as well.''

Longarm didn't even study on that as he tore along the cold gray marble corridor. For he knew who'd killed 'Soos Gomez, but didn't have any notion who'd want to harm good old fat Rhoda!

Chapter 21

Neither naked gal looked her best by the time Longarm and Billy Vail joined them over at the morgue. When folks died in bed, the experienced medical help made sure they'd lay faceup with both hands crossed high on their chest as rigidity set in. Poor old Rhoda had been lying facedown for most of the night by the time they'd found her. So she was all blotched with funny colors down her considerable naked front.

The petite Muskeegee cadaver on the zinc-topped table next to Rhoda's had passed through rigor mortis to lay dishrag limp, with her own lividity showing she'd floated a good ways down the South Platte face-up. Her face was still pretty, despite that big dent above her left eyebrow.

Fat Rhoda had been felled by a hard blow from *her* left as well. But Billy Vail agreed that lots of gents swung blunt objects right-handed, and added, "Them last two gents in the back came in pairs. You reckon they took turns at holding and hitting, or split up to go after those poor gals?"

Longarm said, "There's nothing in the U.S. Constitution saying who had to do what to whom. Pending more expert advice from the autopsy report, I'd say that young whore was killed at least twenty-four hours earlier than Miss Rhoda here. How do you like little Nastassiya well on her way down the river about the time Miss Rhoda and me were meeting up with Glass and Affon at that arcade the night before last?''

Vail shrugged and said, "I don't *like* any of this shit! Are you suggesting this colored Creek child was on that dead Welsh wizard's death list? Whatever for?''

Longarm shook his head. "I don't see how Professor Powers could have ever *met* the pretty little sass. I'm still working on any sensible motive for killing anybody but me. I arrested Powers and I broke up some diabolic plot I still ain't figured out. They might have wanted to shut Dai Jenkins up before he could let me in on it. But why in thunder would they want to kill two gals who didn't even know one another? Rhoda was off duty when I carried Candy Pants Collins and the other two whores over to where Rhoda worked.''

Vail stared soberly down at the dead matron and muttered, "Mayhaps they were afraid this poor beached whale might recognize one or more of them when she did come to work.''

Longarm said, "Don't speak ill of the dead. Miss Rhoda had her faults, but she never deserved to be treated like this.''

Vail cocked a brow and said, "I'd heard she was sweet on you too. What if she was murdered to get back at you?''

Longarm had already thought of that. It didn't make him feel better to have Vail bring it up. He pointed with his chin at the far nicer figure on the other table as he replied, "I never saw this other gal before they killed her. If she was killed before I arrested her pimp, there was just no way they could have expected me to feel bad about a gal I'd never laid eyes on!''

Then he said, "We do have them two other gals connected with the case alive, in better shape to talk. So why don't we see if they can shed some light on the subject.''

Vail stared morosely down at fat Rhoda's mottled cadaver and said, "May as well. Albeit they both swear they ain't seen Nastassiya Nittakechi since she run off with some rich white boy who put a bug in her ear about improving both their lives."

Longarm shook his head and said, "Jealous whores can't tell us a thing they don't know, Billy. I was talking about them other two gals, the doxies Glass and Affon left behind to go gunning for me at that arcade the other night."

Vail started to object, then decided, "The hotel we've put them up at as government witnesses is only a block and a half away. We can't spend the money for fancy hotels on gals who keep saying they don't know nothing."

Longarm said he'd like to try, and warned Billy not to let on that anyone present had gunned the gals' lover boys while he had a word with them.

When they got over to the fleabag hotel near the stockyards, Longarm was glad he'd thought of the stranded drabs. For while neither was a raving beauty, one was a tall dishwater blonde and the other was short and redheaded, save for where she parted her henna-rinsed hair.

The day was warming up, and the gals seemed grateful for the pitcher of spiked lemonade Longarm carried up to their dingy room as a peace offering. Neither gal had been lolling around in more than her chemise. Vail assured them there was no need to dress up for company because he and Longarm were there on business. So the two of them lay back across the one bed, legs crossed, modestly resting on their elbows, while Longarm did the honors with hotel tumblers, explaining as he served them that he already knew they were the ones who'd visited the professor as his sister and daughter.

When he handed her some refreshment, adding that the penalty for lying under oath in a federal court could be considerable, the older and more weatherbeaten blonde asked if there was any way she and her sister in sin might get out of any fool federal hearing.

168

Billy Vail said, "There surely is, ma'am. The professor hung for the murder of those bank examiners. Your boyfriends, Dilwyn Glass and Jack Affon, got killed fair and square trying to carry out the professor's orders the other night. All we have on the two of you is that you had to know a lot more than us about those three dead gents who can't do a thing for either of you now. Your turn."

The henna-rinsed gal sighed and said, "Neither me nor Velma here speak Welsh. Since the two of us have taken time to think back, we just decided that was one of the things they liked about us."

Longarm insisted, "You *were* running messages back and forth between the condemned man and his pals on the outside, though."

The older blonde said, "Sure, we were. But the notes we carried in our teeth so's we could pass them back and forth while kissing the old farts were writ in Welsh, in waterproof ink, on butcher's paper."

Vail said, "Hot damn! Rhoda Bryce was the head matron who should have caught that, but never did, or so she said. They killed Jenkins to shut *him* up too!"

Longarm grimaced and said, "Not on no dead professor's orders. You ladies never went back to visit him after he was hung. So how did your surviving boyfriends get further instructions, in Welsh or any other lingo?"

The henna-rinsed one said, "Plain old U.S. mail, sent care of Denver General Delivery and addressed in plain English with no return address. I seen more than one such envelope, and caught a glimpse of one note to my poor Dilly. It was in Welsh. You can tell because they spell crazy with all those Ys and Ws. I couldn't *pronounce* what the note said. Don't ask me what it *meant*!"

Longarm didn't. He asked what they knew about Candy Pants Collins and his exotic gals. They both acted sincerely astonished, and asked what those Indian whores could have had to offer that *they* couldn't match.

Longarm signaled Vail with his eyes and the older lawman thanked the white gals and told them they'd likely be free to go in a day or so.

Back out on the street, he asked Longarm if he'd just said something dumb.

Longarm said, "Not hardly. I can't make out the whole vessel, but the masts and rigging are commencing to emerge from the mists. Do you mind my taking the rest of the day off to scout for killers, Boss?"

Vail told him he had his blessings. So they shook and parted friendly where the stockyard breezes blew.

Longarm had to ask around, but it didn't take him long to catch up with Knuckles O'Hanlon in another hole-in-the-wall near Cherry Creek. Old Knuckles had rounds to make as he collected tribute and held court for lowlifes who needed fixing.

Knuckles was seated in a booth this time, sipping suds with the owner and a tinhorn gambler called Ace, up from Texas while the law calmed down about a noisy poker game down there.

Longarm didn't sit down as he quietly said, "I got something for you to fix, Fixer. Fix me a charge of criminal conspiracy and murder in the first, with attempted murder of a federal officer thrown in."

Ace almost made a stupid move before O'Hanlon hissed, "Don't even think it, Ace! Allow me to introduce you to the one and original Longarm and praise the Lord you didn't give him the excuse!"

Ace blanched, allowed he was proud to meet up with a gent he'd been told another gent could trust, and politely asked if it was all right for him to go take a leak out back.

The owner said *he* had some chores behind the bar as well. So Longarm and Knuckles were free to talk, and Knuckles lost his amusing brogue.

Knuckles said, "You're barking up the wrong tree. I heard somebody tried to gun you and killed your prisoner instead, not long after we discussed another matter entirely, I told you where you could find Candy Pants and them reservation gals and you found 'em. I don't know toad squat about that Jenkins cuss who was with you the other night.''

Longarm said, "You know who was after me. They didn't have to know my prisoner to nail him with a shot meant for *me*. You didn't tell me where Candy Pants and those *three* young gals were. You told me where I could find a pimp and two whores you hadn't been paid to protect. Then you got word to your rich client. The one who'd hired a sassy young thing who lived up to her nickname of nasty, and he was willing to pay you even more to have me killed before I could really start tracking that one missing gal. So tell me, who paid Tex and Utah to come after me, your whore-beating client himself or you personal?''

Knuckles tried, "I don't know who you're talking about. Nobody on my payroll answers to Tex or, what was that other name, Utah?''

Longarm snapped, "I don't care what you *call* the one in the Texas sombrero. He was seated at the table playing cards with you the other night.''

Knuckles blinked and said, "No, he wasn't! He wasn't even on the premises—''

Then he caught himself, sighed, and said, "That was mighty sneaky. So what kind of a deal could this child still hope to make with you? It ain't as if Tex and Utah *won*, you know.''

Longarm said, "Somebody killed a federal want and a lady I was fond of. I want him. You give him to me and we never had this conversation. You hold out on me and you have my word I'll kill you and call it resisting arrest. You know I have enough to connect Tex and Utah to both you and their attempt to murder me. So that ought to stand up at the coroner's inquest, and you have to my count of ten to make up your damned mind!''

It didn't take Knuckles O'Hanlon that long. He only asked if they might part friendly in return for some friendly advice. Once Longarm grudgingly agreed he could go along

171

with that, Knuckles O'Hanlon told him, "You want a slick lawyer named Graystone, Murgatroid Graystone, Esquire. He's a pillar of the community and a total degenerate who likes to poke colored kids up the ass. You guessed right about that reservation gal being nasty. When he set her up in a luxurious home of her own and tried to give her a Greek lesson, she scratched him good and he clobbered her with a lamp before he came to me, all bloody-cheeked and worried sick. He seemed more worried about folks finding out he liked dark meat then he was about the killing. I sent Tex and old Utah to help him tidy up. They told me later about dumping her in the river. I never would have let them dispose of her so dumb. If Graystone paid them to go after you, they never let me in on it. I would have advised against it. You proved my point when they came after you. I reckon that was after I told them you'd made me hand over the other Indian gals. Being a slippery lawyer, Graystone likely worried about the whole thing coming out as you kept scouting for the one left over. You do have a rep for scouting and, like I said, he's a lawyer who'd know better than most which lawmen a man might want to worry about after he clobbers a play-pretty."

Longarm grimaced, and asked how the killing of fat Rhoda might fit in with a whore-killing lawyer's cover-up.

Knuckles O'Hanlon sounded sincere as he replied, "I don't know. I swear I never gave my blessings to the killing of anybody. I'm a fixer. I'm not a professional assassin. Tex and Utah were fools to go after a gunslick with your rep. So how about it, are we pals again?"

Longarm said, "Not hardly. But I couldn't run you out of town without making your precinct captain cry. So just don't ever hold out on me like that again and we'll say no more about it."

He ignored the hand the fixer held out to him, and grumped out of the dinky saloon to head northeast toward the state capitol grounds. He knew Lawyer Graystone on sight, and the best place to find such a cuss at this hour of the day would be around the state courts, where such rascals spent more time making deals in the halls than in their offices or trying cases in court.

As luck would have it, Murgatroid Graystone, Esquire was jawing with Reporter Crawford from the *Denver Post* in the capitol rotunda under the dome as Longarm entered from the south hallway. As he approached, the Lincoln-esque lawyer in black spotted him, and didn't wait to be be told a thing before he went for the shoulder holster under his own frock coat.

Longarm yelled, "Crawford! Get out of my way!" as the normally very dignified legal eagle got his Police Special .38 out with a red-faced snarl of animal rage.

But the burly Reporter Crawford had a better idea, and grabbed Graystone's wrist with both hands as the hissing lawyer spanged a .38 slug off the marble floor near Longarm's advancing boots.

Then Longarm had pistol-whipped the raging lawyer senseless, and a heavier Reporter Crawford wound up on top of him, taking his smoking gun away from him as he stared up at Longarm to ask, "Why did I just jump this poor gent, pard?"

Longarm said, "He wasn't no gent. He was a disgusting brute who beat women to death when they wouldn't let him corn-hole them. But let me get these cuffs on him before he wakes up and I'll be proud to tell you his sad story. For it was in hopes of keeping his secret life out of the newspapers that he committed murder most foul and paid other assholes to come after me!"

Crawford beamed and chortled, "Hot damn! What a scoop! Does that mean I just helped you solve the mystery of the dead chess master's devious doings at last?"

To which Longarm could only reply. "Not hardly. Only half of it. I still have another arrest to make before the professor and me can call it a stalemate, which is chess talk for a dumb draw."

Chapter 22

A slick lawyer with connections had slick lawyers with connections. So it took a lot of hemming, hawing, and wires back and forth by the time the city, state, and two federal districts agreed the son of a bitch would have to stand trial at Fort Smith for the murder of little Nastassiya Nittakechi of the Creek Reserve.

It seemed a shame to Longarm that the proud pervert wouldn't get to stand trial in front of his high-toned Denver neighbors, as he'd feared. But on the other hand, Judge Isaac Parker was as willing to hang a white man for murdering an Indian as an Indian for murdering a white man. So what the hell.

They got Murgatroid Graystone, Esquire, locked up in the cell next to that of Candy Pants Collins about eight that evening. Pop Wetzel allowed it wouldn't hurt if they just cussed one another at a safe distance until those Fort Smith deputies showed up to carry them both back to see Judge Parker.

It was sort of amusing as a whore-monger and a whore-beater wracked their brains for dirty names to call one another. Longarm waited until he was out front alone with the boss turnscrew before he said, "I'd be obliged if you told Stubby Sheen, when he comes on in the morning, that I don't think Lawyer Graystone had anything to do with the murder of Rhoda Bryce."

Pop said, "It's likely just as well for Lawyer Graystone then. Rhoda had friends here in both wings. Who do you reckon killed her if it wasn't Graystone?"

Longarm said, "One of Professor Powers's gang. Rhoda helped me when them last two Welshmen came after me. Billy Vail and me were talking to their doxies, the ones who visited Professor Powers to run messages back and forth. They kept getting messages in Welsh after Professor Powers was dead. I've about narrowed things down to a few bare possibles. So I'm expecting to make an important arrest within twenty-four hours."

As Pop walked Longarm out front, he said, "Well, we got plenty of room in the back. But didn't somebody tell me there was thirteen names on that list Stubby found? I make that only nine Welshmen and a Mexican accounted for so far."

Longarm said, "Those last two weren't Welshmen. Others may not be really in on any plot. We can't seem to locate some of those names on any yellow sheets at all. They might not all exist. Professor Powers made a heap of wild statements on his way to the gallows, and he might have put down thirteen names just to be spooky. Dai Jenkins swore to the last he didn't know any Professor Powers. Lord knows how many of the other gun waddies did."

Pop scowled and said, "Aw, come on. Why did all them jaspers want to kill you for the professor if they didn't know the professor?"

Longarm said, "I mean to ask when I catch the one still sending out messages in Welsh. I suspect most of those outlaws were only told I was on to them and coming after them. Would you really care who sent you such a warning in Welsh if you were a Welsh-talking outlaw with a lot of other worries on your mind?"

Pop decided, "I reckon not. So are you saying the professor never *had* no real gang? He was only trying to pay you back by telling you where you might find a wanted outlaw, then warning that wanted outlaw you were coming for him?"

Longarm nodded grimly and replied, "It almost worked, didn't it? I wasted a heap of time trying to figure out how a con man might use a bunch of dull-witted gun slingers to swindle a bank. Then I noticed it made more sense that a Welsh-speaking crook of any kind would be likely to keep a mental record of other Welshmen he'd met along the owlhoot trail, in jail and so on. A Welsh gal I learned not to trust too much assured me Welsh folks trust one another more than they trust the rest of us. So, keeping a list of Welsh-reading crooks, then writing to 'em in Welsh to warn them about a lawman they'd been betrayed to . . ."

"I follow your drift," Pop Wetzel said adding with an impish grin that he was sure glad he wasn't Welsh.

Longarm grinned just as impishly when he said, "I know you ain't. Our office clerk and a Welsh-speaking deputy have been going over our old job applications. I was surprised to see your mother came from the Basque Country of Spain, though, no offense."

Pop said, "None taken. My late momma was *proud* of being Basque."

So they shook out front and parted friendly. Longarm went back to that same fleabag hotel and had a private talk with the night clerk. They got a lot of business from the Denver District Court and wanted more. So it was simple for Longarm to wrangle a free room for the night across the hall from those two material witnesses, with neither the blonde nor the henna-head aware he was there.

Nobody called on either during the course of the night. Nobody called on Longarm because he hadn't told anybody but the room clerk he might be spending the night there.

Come morning, he left without either gal knowing he'd been watching over them through the night. He enjoyed a hearty breakfast, and went on over to the Federal Building to see if any radishes had sprouted overnight.

Some had. Western Union had helped them track down Glynnis Mathry. She was in Boston trying to sell her book about the Wild West. It seemed unlikely she'd been writing in Welsh to Wild West killers. Why she'd stolen that list was one of those unanswered questions, like why some high-society ladies stole napkins or salt shakers when you invited them to tea. Longarm scratched her off as a frisky gal with a peculiar streak.

They took their own good time scratching others off the list of possible suspects. For as Billy Vail kept warning, you had to get rid of the ones it couldn't possibly be. You didn't want to throw one dish out with the dishwater. So it was late that afternoon when Longarm got the warrant he needed from Henry and went over to the Black Cat Saloon.

The first time he peered through the swinging doors, the man that he wanted wasn't there. He cussed and circled over to the railroad station and back. The next time he tried, a lean young jasper wearing a riding outfit and a double-action Remington .44-40 was nursing his beer against the bar.

Longarm strode boldly in and said, "You'd best let me have that six-gun. I see no need to cuff you, since it's only a short walk to the House of Detention, Evan Pew."

The slightly shorter and far skinnier cuss at the bar unbuckled his gun rig without argument, but asked if he might see the warrant for his arrest. Longarm told him, not unkindly, "You can read it once we get to the lockup. I want to sign you in before sundown and the tricky light of gloaming."

So they left the saloon like old pals as the barkeep whispered to another customer, "Did you see that? Smooth as a mill pond, without a sign of resistance!"

The customer shrugged and said, "I'd have gone quiet too. They say he can treat you sort of rough if you sass him."

So a few minutes later Longarm marched his latest arrest

into the federal House of Detention, his own gun grips exposed as he casually carried the younger man's gun rig over his left forearm.

They found that ash-blond matron seated at Stubby Sheen's usual desk. Longarm smiled uncertainly down at her and asked, "Ain't you still pulling night duty in the women's wing, Miss Roxanne?"

The head matron demurely replied, "We've had to shuffle since your sweetheart, Rhoda, was murdered. Stubby's in the back, warning Candy Pants what will happen to him if he keeps screaming like that. What have we here?"

Longarm nodded at the younger man and told her, "Even Pew from Welsh Wales out of Kansas. I ain't certain what he's done, but his name was on that list the professor left us. So Billy Vail figures he's good for seventy-two on suspicion."

The kid called Evan Pew protested, "I ain't done anything. I ain't done nothing wrong to man or beast, and I'm fixing to sue you all for false arrest!"

Stubby Sheen came out to join them, muttering about pimps who needed more cocaine than the taxpayers were about to buy for them in a durned old federal lockup.

Longarm repeated what he'd just told Roxanne Rawlston about the kid he wanted to hold. Stubby shot the prisoner a keen look and asked, "You sure you know what you're doing, Longarm? We had us an Evan Pew in the back last summer. Had to let him go on a writ, but they said he was bad news with a six-gun. I mind the cuss well, and this ain't him."

Longarm shrugged and said, "He'll have to do until the real Pew comes along then. I don't write up these fool warrants. I only get to serve them."

He handed Henry's typed-up warrant over. Stubby read it, shrugged, and said, "Well, Mr. Pew, it's your misfortune and none of my own."

He opened his ledger, copied the vital statistics off the warrant, and added, "Let's find you a nice cell in the back.

I'd say a nice *quiet* cell, but we've got a pimp crying for cocaine and a weeping disgraced lawyer back there, and it figures to be a long night."

As the three of them started back, Stubby added, "I'm glad I'll be going off duty soon. Will you hold the fort for me until I finish putting this one to bed, Miss Roxanne?"

She allowed she'd be proud to. With Stubby leading the way and Longarm bringing up the rear, the three of them strode into the gloomy corridor leading to the cell blocks, with their prisoner bitching that he hadn't eaten yet.

As Stubby led the way to a cell door Evan Pew asked him casually, *"Pa bryd y maer swper?"*

So Stubby answered without thinking, *"Chwech o'r gloch."*

Then Stubby Sheen froze, blanched, and demanded, *"Er mwyn Mari! Pwy yw hwn?"*

So "Evan Pew" turned to Longram and calmy remarked, "I asked him what time we ate back here and he said six o'clock. Then he asked for the sake of Mary what was going on."

Longarm nodded agreeably and said, "This here prisoner is really U.S. Deputy Marshal Dewey, Stubby. He's new here in Denver, so I was hoping you'd accept him as just a dumb Welsh kid and feel sorry enough for him to be off your guard."

Stubby tried, "Off my guard about what? So my folks split up when I was little and a Welsh grandmother raised me. Was that against the law?"

"Lying to a federal officer in the course of a criminal trackdown is sure as hell against the law," said Longarm cheerfully enough. "The professor was only talking wild. He never wrote no list. It was *you* who made it up, while I was sitting the death watch with the poor old cuss. You put down the names of men *he* never laid eyes on! Killers or would-be killers you'd met and gossiped with in Welsh as they was passing through."

Then he shrugged and asked, "Why am I telling you all

this? It was your own grand notion. You know how you worked your way into the confidence of those two local gunslicks the professor was smuggling notes to, hoping they might be able to save his neck some way. How did you get them to come after me at that arcade? And don't say I never told you I'd been assigned to that arcade to catch Candy Pants Collins. Rhoda told me you'd told her I'd be there, lucky for me.''

Stubby was staring thoughtfully at the pistol grips jutting up from the gun rig over Longarm's left forearm as he stammered, ''Sure, I told Rhoda where I thought you'd be. She asked me. Was it my fault the gal was hot for you, damn it?''

Longarm sofly answered, ''It was her business who she admired more than you, Stubby. Is that how come you killed her, once she came back here bragging that she'd seduced me at last?''

Stubby grabbed for the gun grips, seeing Deputy Dewey was unarmed and Longarm's .44-40 was partly blocked by the dangling gun rig. But Longarm had suspected he might try that. So he just took his time to draw and throw down as the desperate turnkey clicked the hammer of Dewey's empty gun twice more, then dropped it and fumbled with his covered army holster.

So Longarm pistol-whipped him against the bars, and Dewey caught him from behind as he bounced, pinning his arms to his sides as he cussed them just dreadfully in Welsh.

Longarm unbuckled Stubby's gunbelt and let it fall to the cement as he told Dewey, ''I'd say we got more than enough on him now, wouldn't you, pard?''

Dewey said they sure did as Roxanne Rawlston came warily back to see what all the fuss was about.

She naturally asked how come Longarm seemed to be helping a prisoner attack the boss turnkey. So Longarm explained, ''We're arresting Stubby for criminal conspiracy and murder, Miss Roxanne. His motive was as old as time.

180

He lusted for a lady who refused to hold hands with him and kept expressing admiration for another man.''

The better-looking blonde stared owl-eyed at Stubby and told them, "Everyone was laughing about him and Rhoda. Nobody knew he felt *that* serious! You say he was the one who went over to her carriage house to murder her?''

Longarm sighed and said, "Let's get him in one of these cells. We can work out the details later. He's just proven he has homicidal tendencies to go with his mastery of a tough lingo!''

So they searched Stubby, and locked him up as he cussed them all in English. Roxanne glared through the bars at him and said if it had been up to her, she'd have killed him and saved the taxpayers a trial.

Longarm told her, "He was likely trying to commit suicide just now, ma'am. But I didn't feel I owed him any favors. You and the rest of Miss Rhoda's friends will have the pleasure of his company for as long as it takes to try him and hang him right out back.''

The pretty head matron suddenly beamed at Longarm and declared, "Rhoda was right about you, Custis! You *do* have brains to match those wide shoulders! But look, the night shift will be relieving me any time now, and you've barely begun to explain all this to me. So I know this swell Chinese place right here in the neighborhood, and—''

Longarm cut in to suggest a fancy French restaurant even closer. He wasn't about to let that pretty waitress at the Golden Dragon see him with another gal as pretty as old Roxanne.